MELANCHOLY HARMONIES

By

Jeanine Banza-Katungutere

Copyright © 2026 by Jeanine Banza-Katungutere.
All rights reserved.

This book is a work of nonfiction or fiction. Any resemblance to actual persons, living or dead, or actual events is purely coincidental.

No part of this publication may be reproduced, stored in a retrieval system, or transmitted in any form or by any means without the prior written permission of the author, except for brief quotations used in reviews.

ISBN: 979-8-9936380-0-3

FOREWORD

Human experience is a journey marked by highs and lows, pain, loss, and wounds, sometimes invisible, yet always profound. At the heart of these trials, we seek comfort, light, and a path to heal what has been broken.

I am a trained legal professional, a father of fifteen children, a grandfather to many grandchildren, and a great-grandfather to my great-great-grandchildren. Today, I speak to you with deep conviction: it is long past time to reform our approach to emotional, relational, and sexual education.

This book dares to break the silence surrounding a still-taboo subject and has the potential to become a vital tool in preventing moral and sexual abuse, tragedies that cause immense physical and emotional suffering.

Our children, and future generations, must understand the humanitarian damage inflicted by humans upon other humans. Crimes against humanity, often silenced by reckless ambitions and the thirst to invade, violate, and neutralize those who are supposed to be protected, must stop. Where is the justice that should rise like dawn after endless nights of darkness, to ensure that light prevails?

The author of this book, driven by a desire to break the taboo surrounding conversations about sex, takes us on a journey where melancholy yields to a gentle melody, one of rebuilding and reconciliation with what was violently shattered.

It is a path marked by storms and pouring rain, intertwined with tears from a weary heart burdened by unspoken pain and suffering.

I recommend to current and future generations that they use this moving narrative, *"Melancholy Harmonies,"* as a bridge to break down taboos and generational shame. It is urgent to protect human dignity and rights, and to no longer deny these genuine emotions that deserve recognition. This book offers us the opportunity to reopen silenced conversations, those that have been muted but have nonetheless caused harm across generations, now igniting a forest fire.

It should serve to revive the discussions of yesterday, those our ancestors once held around the fire by moonlight, reimagined for our modern world. I invite you, with all the strength of my heart, to read this book and to share it with your children and grandchildren, in schools, churches, and within families. Let it become a tool for change, a voice against forgetfulness, a shield against indifference.

This book is a powerful call for justice, truth, and the recognition of authentic emotions. Let us not allow shame to continue killing in the shadows. Together, let us open dialogue, break the silence, and build a future where every human being can live with dignity and safety.

From suffering, the strongest souls are born. The most resilient characters bear the scars of their wounds.

I warmly recommend this book. Read it, share it, and encourage others to do the same. Because it is through speaking out that justice will finally rise.

HONORÉ MULUMBA KALALA NJINGULULA

Writer and author,

Democratic Republic of the Congo.

FOREWORD

There are works that deliberately bring to the surface memories buried deep within the subconscious, much like this one. Bukavu, November 1998. At that time, in my professional capacity, I had to listen to the testimonies of women who were victims of torture and rape, women carrying the scars of violence endured during an ongoing armed conflict in eastern Democratic Republic of the Congo, which continues to inflict immeasurable suffering. *"Harmonies of Melancholy"* evoked in me the same overwhelming feeling of sadness.

This book is a poignant account that plunges the reader into a profound truth: that of sexual abuse, a social and mental pathology. It gnaws at society, spreading like the neurotoxin of the black mamba, a venom that acts on the nervous system and quickly causes paralysis of the respiratory muscles. This venom was injected into the main character, Nyota, a young woman whose journey is profoundly upheaved.

Originating from an unstable geopolitical zone, the Democratic Republic of the Congo, Nyota and her parents were forced to migrate to the United States to escape armed conflict and the visible and invisible traumas endured by those responsible for her safety. After being forced to perform inappropriate acts during her childhood, the rest of her childhood and adolescence were marked by major personal challenges that no child should ever have to endure.

In the labyrinth of the human soul, where the remnants of the past intertwine with the promise of a possible future, lies a universal truth: suffering does not necessarily guarantee the future we hope for. Will it lose its weight or crush the heroine, Nyota? Whatever the outcome, *"Harmonies of Melancholy"* raises essential questions, including the persistence of taboos surrounding sexual and moral violence, emotional and sexual education, war, immigration, and many others that you will discover throughout this compelling journey.

I would like to commend the courage of Jeanine Banza Katungutere who, by sharing this story inspired by real events, offers a valuable tool to parents, educators, and survivors. The ubiquity of predators is frightening, but we must confront them with unwavering determination. Simply put, danger is at our doorstep, and no one should remain silent. To ensure this story reaches a wide audience, in homes, schools, and communities, it is crucial to raise awareness among children on this subject.

This novel, told with extraordinary clarity and delicacy, is a striking blend of optimism and irony that poetically depicts the multifaceted cruelty of human nature. A revelation!

Maguy Kabamba
Translator and Writer.

What I read made me cry.

Thirty years of dreadful war, unspeakable and merciless in its scope and devastation. Thirty years spent trying to bring to life a wild, utopian dream—a mere chimera—that, on the contrary, shatters the dream of an entire generation, sowing desolation and deeply anchoring hatred within it, to the point of questioning whether peaceful coexistence between the two peoples will ever again be possible. A hypothetical coexistence seriously compromised in light of the legendary Congolese hospitality of yesteryear, which is now paid for in ingratitude by these Tutsi warlords for over thirty years...

In this story, Madame Jeanine Banza plays on multiple levels, weaving abundant suspense. This makes her narrative somewhat mysterious and captivating. The story has the merit of describing a nearly universal tragedy—killings, lies, hatred—spanning a long thirty-year war on the populations of Kivu, without losing hope that one day peace will return. Thirty years of war, enough now, monsieur Paul Kagame!

EMMANUEL MER, Wiseman, KIVU

TABLE OF CONTENTS

FOREWORD iii

ACKNOWLEDGEMENT xii

DEDICATION xiii

PREFACE xi

CHAPTER 1 1

    When the War Arrived in the Mailbox 1

CHAPTER 2 15

    The Child the Ancestors Heard 15

CHAPTER 3 25

    The Night the Boots Turned Back 25

CHAPTER 4 39

    The Country Where Nothing Is Free 39

CHAPTER 5 57

    The Song That Drew the Wolf 57

CHAPTER 6 78

    Nyota Despised Herself 78

CHAPTER 7	103
The Day the Silence Spoke	103
CHAPTER 8	159
When Healing Took Her Hand	159
EPILOGUE	181
REFERENCES	186
ABOUT THE AUTHOR	187

ACKNOWLEDGEMENT

My special gratitude goes to Nyota, who allowed her story to be told to prevent further sexual harm to humanity caused by sexual abuse. I would not have found the courage to shake myself free from the taboo I grew up with, nor to become passionate about teaching children, had I not listened to her story.

DEDICATION

I dedicate this book to every girl or boy who has been a victim of sexual abuse. You are special and uniquely designed for greatness.

Jeanine Banza Katungutere

Author and storyteller, mother,

and a child life coach to children, teens, and young adults.

In Tender Memory

To Archbishop Christophe Munzihirwa Mwene Ngabo (1926–1996), Archbishop of Bukavu. A shepherd who chose to stay with his flock in their darkest hour. A man of faith and courage who spoke out when others remained silent. A martyr.

Archbishop Munzihirwa urged the people of Bukavu not to flee in fear, but to stand firm and resist the invaders. His voice, his presence, and his unwavering call to justice gave hope to a city on the brink.

On the afternoon of October 29, 1996, he was shot and killed after Rwandan soldiers attacked him. His body was left lying in the open street for over 24 hours before a group of seminarians dared to recover his remains.

His sacrifice is not forgotten. His voice still echoes.

This book is dedicated, in part, to his memory.

PREFACE

The statistics on child sexual abuse and human trafficking are deeply alarming, revealing a pervasive issue that remains vastly underreported worldwide. According to the World Health Organization, globally, about one in five women and one in seven men report experiencing sexual abuse during childhood. In the United States alone, at least one in four girls and approximately one in twenty boys have experienced sexual abuse or assault before reaching adulthood.

These figures, already staggering, are considered only the tip of the iceberg due to extensive underreporting. Research suggests that between 70% and 90% of child sexual abuse incidents are never reported to authorities, often due to fear, shame, or the victim's relationship with the perpetrator. Indeed, about 85% to 90% of perpetrators are individuals known and trusted by the child, including family members, teachers, coaches, or religious leaders. Even more disturbingly, approximately 30% to 40% of perpetrators are juveniles themselves, often continuing a tragic cycle of abuse.

The consequences of this trauma are profound and lasting. Victims of child sexual abuse face significantly increased risks of mental health disorders, including depression, anxiety, and PTSD. They are also at higher risk for substance abuse, risky sexual behavior, and chronic physical health conditions such as heart disease and obesity. Tragically, women who have experienced childhood sexual abuse are two to thirteen times more likely to be sexually victimized again in adulthood, illustrating the devastating cycle of revictimization.

On a global scale, child trafficking further compounds the severity of the issue. The International Labour Organization estimates that, at any given time, 3.3 million children are victims of forced labor, with more than 1.5 million specifically subjected to commercial sexual exploitation. Recent reports indicate a troubling rise: child trafficking increased by 31% from 2019 to 2022. This rise includes sexual exploitation, forced labor, and forced criminal activities, highlighting a global emergency that requires urgent and comprehensive action.

Despite increased awareness and some progress in prosecution rates, conviction rates remain worryingly low. In the U.S., federal prosecutions have risen, with 1,656 trafficking defendants prosecuted in fiscal year 2022, yet the vast majority of abuses still never result in justice. Globally, convictions for human trafficking offenses fell by 27% from 2019 to 2020, reflecting substantial challenges in enforcement and accountability.

These stark statistics underline a crucial need for greater awareness, prevention, intervention, and support for survivors. Without substantial improvements in reporting, prosecution, and victim support systems, the devastating cycle of child abuse and exploitation will persist, continuing to impact millions of lives around the world.

And yet, the world continues to turn a blind eye.

In the midst of all this, pornography thrives. The industry is valued at approximately ninety-seven billion dollars. In 2019 alone, a single porn website, Porn-hub, received around forty-two billion visitors. That's more than five times the total human population. When the world shut down during the COVID-19 pandemic, those numbers skyrocketed. People were locked inside, isolated, searching for escape, and pornography was there, waiting.

For years, experts have warned about the impact of pornography, especially on young minds. It distorts perceptions of sex, blurring the lines between fantasy and reality. It desensitizes people to violence, conditioning them to see degradation and exploitation as normal, even desirable. And it is, undeniably, a gateway.

Many victims of human trafficking report that their abusers first introduced them to pornography as children, using it to groom them, to break them, to prepare them for what was coming. Parents are beginning to wake up to the dangers their children face. In the United States and Europe, more conversations are being had about the importance of sex education—teaching children about consent, about safe and unsafe touch.

But at the same time, children are being exposed to sexual content at an alarming rate. The very thing parents are trying to protect them from is slipping through the cracks, finding them through the internet, through social media, through the entertainment industry. It is being normalized. Sanitized. Wrapped up in messages of empowerment and freedom, making it all the more insidious.

For children who experience abuse or are exposed to sexual content too early, the effects are profound. The damage is not just physical. It is emotional, psychological, and spiritual. It carves deep wounds into their sense of self, into their understanding of love and intimacy. It steals their innocence, sometimes before they even realize what has been taken from them.

For many parents, especially those from conservative or religious backgrounds, the idea of discussing sex with their children is terrifying. It is awkward, uncomfortable, sometimes even shameful. In some cultures, it is considered taboo, something to be whispered about in hushed tones—if it is spoken about at all. But silence has never protected anyone. Silence is the very thing that abusers rely on. It is their shield, their weapon.

Stories have always been a powerful tool for teaching. Across all cultures, all generations, storytelling has been the way we pass down wisdom, the way we explain the unexplainable. And now, more than ever, we need stories that speak the truth. Stories that shine a light on the darkness. Stories that equip children with the knowledge they need to protect themselves.

Proper, age-appropriate sex education is not about corrupting children. It is about safeguarding them. It is about ensuring they understand what is safe and what is not, what is love and what is control, what is natural and what is manipulation. It is about breaking the cycle of silence that has allowed abuse to flourish for centuries.

To do this, we must be willing to confront the barriers that have been placed in our way. Cultural shame. Religious stigma. Generational silence. These things do not protect children; they leave them vulnerable. By refusing to talk about sex, we are handing the conversation over to predators, to the media, to a society that is more interested in profit than in protection. God created sex with purpose. It was never meant to be twisted, distorted, or weaponized.

Yet that is exactly what has happened. By keeping these conversations hidden, we are not protecting the sanctity of what God designed—we are allowing the enemy to take control of it. We are letting the abusers win.

I pray that the story of Nyota sparks conversations. That it opens the door for parents and children to speak honestly, to recognize the dangers that are so often hidden in plain sight. The media, the internet, the content children consume daily—so much of it carries messages they do not yet have the tools to understand. Schools are introducing teachings that blur moral lines. Even within families, even within churches, not everyone can be trusted.

This is not just a book. It is a call to awareness. A plea to break the silence before another child falls victim to a world that is built to strip them of their innocence.

It is time to take back the conversation.

Melancholy Harmonies

Chapter 1

When the War Arrived in the Mailbox

Bibi wasn't expecting the letter to arrive so soon. She stood barefoot at the mailbox in her bathrobe and night bonnet, her hands slick with nerves as she rifled through postcards, flyers, and a dreaded stack of unpaid bills. Her heart stuttered when she spotted a blue stamp from the Texas Department of Criminal Justice.

It sliced through her like a hidden blade. *Not today,* she thought. *Not before the bride price ceremony.* She had been hoping the infamous letter would wait until after the weekend so she could enjoy, just a little, the sweetness of life.

Her wig still hadn't arrived either, another thing rattling her patience. It was the first time she had ever ordered one online, persuaded by her daughter Nyota to "just try it." The plan was to have it styled before Saturday, when the president of their local Congolese community would be giving away his eldest daughter in marriage. Bibi didn't even know if she would be stable enough to attend. Online shopping and tracking numbers made her anxious. But if Nyota said it was the modern way, then she wanted to try, if only to impress her child. Still, in moments like this, she wished she had gone to a store as she used to.

Clutching the mail against her chest, she slipped back inside and tossed the pile onto the hallway table without looking too closely. She tried to ignore it, the way she sometimes pretended she hadn't seen painful news. But her eyes betrayed her. There it was again, that blue stamp she remembered from Lisa's warning. She could almost hear Lisa's sharp voice, telling her what the outside of the letter would look like. Suddenly, she was pacing from the living room to the bedroom, up the stairs, then back down again, checking the window in case Nyota appeared and found her in this disarray. She had wanted to seem calm before Nyota returned. Strong. Not like this.

Her legs carried her toward the bathroom. She didn't know whether she needed to vomit or urinate. *Diarrhea? Impossible. I haven't eaten anything,* she thought. Splashing water on her face, she leaned over the sink and stared into her own frightened eyes. *It's only a letter,* she told herself silently. *Just a letter. Why does it shake me like this?*

She whispered a prayer she had prayed so many times before: "In Jesus' name, spirit of fear, leave me…"

Tears rose anyway. Silent tears, hot and humiliating. *I don't want Nyota to suffer anymore,* she pleaded inwardly. *Lord, delete this from our memory. Bring deliverance.* She remembered someone once telling her that crying was good, that tears unclogged old grief. So she let herself cry, not just for herself but for her daughter too, clutching the half-open letter in her moist palm.

The first line of the letter burned into her mind even before she spoke it aloud:

*"Dear Bibi and Tatu,
You are registered in the confidential and integrated victim notification system..."*

She stopped there, chest pounding.

Tatu came home from work to find her frozen in place, as if rooted to the floor, the letter still clutched in her trembling hands.

"What's wrong, Bibi? You look shaken," he said gently.

She didn't reply immediately. When she finally spoke, her voice came out brittle. "We are registered... in the victim notification system..."

She couldn't finish the sentence. All at once, time seemed to freeze around her. Questions that had no answers pressed against her heart: *Can the wounds of childhood sexual violence ever be healed? When will this cycle of butchery that haunts one generation to the next finally end? Will we ever receive a letter of justice, not one of warning, but one of apology? One where the words read: 'Sincere regrets...'? Will that day ever come?*

Bibi stood there, suspended between hope and despair, knowing the letter in her grip could carry either mercy or another tidal wave of pain.

***

Far away from her immaculate kitchen and trembling hands lay the soil that birthed all this sorrow.

Kahuzi-Biega National Park, nestled in the heart of the eastern Democratic Republic of the Congo, is a sanctuary unlike any other, a lush, breathing relic of Earth's ancient rhythms. Cradled near the city of Bukavu, not far from the Rwandan border and just twenty miles from the glittering expanse of Lake Kivu, the park is a miracle of survival in a country scarred by endless wars. Its name comes from two

Melancholy Harmonies

sleeping giants, Mount Kahuzi and Mount Biega, dormant volcanoes rising like silent sentinels above the canopy, their stoic presence bearing witness to generations of struggle.

Once, this land thrived untouched, a paradise where whispers of the jungle swallowed the noise of the outside world. For centuries, it lived to its own quiet pulse, seemingly indifferent to the bloodshed and shifting borders unraveling around it. But war is a slow cancer. It creeps through broken politics, slips across fraying frontiers, draining even the most sacred places of their peace. Today, the stillness of the forest hides a hum of tension that seems to throb beneath every leaf and stone.

The mighty gorillas that once ruled this territory, heavy-bellied guardians with wise eyes and human-like hands, now exist under constant threat. Poachers lurk in the shadows, and soldiers march where tourists once tread. Even now, the park keeps breathing. Its tangled green refuses to surrender. Somehow, its beauty persists, as if daring the violence to erase it completely.

Visitors continue to arrive, courageous souls searching for something rare and undefiled. They hope to glimpse the gorillas, yes, but also to witness something much more elusive: purity, resilience, a fragment of goodness in a world hooked on decay.

Lake Kivu sprawls nearby like a glimmering emerald wound, breathtaking and lethal in the same breath. Beneath its jeweled surface lies a volatile secret: a monstrous reservoir of methane and carbon dioxide, trapped in ancient pockets of water from centuries of volcanic eruptions. Scientists call it a "sleeping beast." If those gases ever ruptured in a limnic explosion, as happened decades ago in Cameroon, death would race across the land like a choking tide. And yet the people remain. They farm. They fish. They build homes along its edges. The land is too generous, too rich to abandon. It demands everything, and yet it gives everything in return.

But beauty in the Congo is a double-edged sword. Beneath its soil lie treasures the world cannot resist: gold, tin, cobalt, coltan, the glittering veins that power modern life. If you own a phone, a laptop, a car, then you carry a sliver of this cursed earth in your hands. Congo bleeds into every pocket, every screen. Its wealth is the seed of its suffering.

Melancholy Harmonies

Foreign armies, rebel militias, and mercenaries masquerading as saviors all crave what sleeps under the ground. So they dig, they kill, they take.

In the 1990s and early 2000s, eastern Congo became a theater of horrors that defied the imagination. This was not war in the conventional sense. It was a harvest of bodies. A slaughter engineered not to conquer, but to erase. In response, a group of traditional warriors, the Mai-Mai, rose up in defiance. Cloaked in rituals and legend, they were revered across the region as much for their mystical powers as for their weapons. Stories circulated that bullets slid off their skin like drops of water, that they could vanish into smoke. Myth or morale, no one could tell, but the tales gave them courage. They stood boldly against M23 rebels and encroaching Rwandan troops.

Over time, they adopted a new name: Wazalendo, meaning "true patriots," in Swahili. They were no longer rebels. They were the heartbeat of a people refusing to vanish.

Yet wars evolve. They grow old and cynical. They break men and swallow heroes.

By 2025, a new generation of Wazalendo had risen, not seasoned warriors, but the children of the dead. Orphans sculpted into fighters, born in the ashes of torched villages, raised in sprawling refugee camps, fed on injustice and exile. Many had never tasted peace. They carried rifles the way other children carried notebooks. Boys with fractured smiles. Girls with embers burning behind their eyes. They were not rebels. They were vengeance embodied.

For years they were dismissed, labeled criminals, troublemakers, shadows on the periphery. The president before Félix Tshisekedi ignored their warnings as foreign powers stripped the land like carrion feeders. But Tshisekedi saw them differently. He saw sons and daughters of the Congo. He gave them recognition and purpose. Under his leadership, the Wazalendo were woven into the national army, the Forces Armées de la République Démocratique du Congo (FARDC). Together, they formed a living wall against the darkness. They fought to hold provinces long surrendered to chaos. They guarded villages forgotten by their own government and abandoned by the world.

They were no longer rebels. They were the heartbeat of a people refusing to vanish.

But resistance demands blood.

The invaders' strategy was brutally simple: destabilize, erase, empty the land until it could be seized without resistance. Those who remained paid the price in flesh. Terror was not a by-product; it was the weapon. Mass rape became a tool of war, engineered to fracture communities from the inside out. It did more than destroy bodies; it severed bloodlines. In places where children should have grown, only silence took root.

Men, women, even the smallest children, were targeted, humiliated, annihilated. When people were too broken to fight, they fled. And once they fled, their land lay exposed, ripe for conquest.

This was documented in reports and testimonies. The names behind the atrocities were not hidden. Critics of Paul Kagame, President of Rwanda, and his general, James Kabarebe, allege that their policies and support for armed groups devastated eastern Congo.

And Kagame was not alone. Uganda, China, Europe, and the United States all played their parts. They did not need to pull triggers; they only needed to stay silent while the minerals streamed outward like veins drained from a body. There were UN briefings.

Whistleblowers. Mountains of evidence. Still, nothing changed. Kagame continued to sell looted Congolese minerals to the highest bidders, amassing wealth brick by brick atop a foundation of corpses. And the world bought, gladly.

Yet in the darkness, a few voices refused to be silenced. President Félix Tshisekedi, Congo's fifth head of state since independence, spoke bluntly on the global stage, naming names and calling for sanctions.

Mockers said he was threatening when he declared from Goma, *"A partir ya Goma, tokosimba Kigali wana,"* meaning "From Goma, we will touch Kigali." The line was widely mocked. Nevertheless, despite everything happening behind the scenes or out in the open, he was among the first recent leaders to speak this bluntly about the Rwandan president. What followed stirred concern among multinationals. But it was far from the end of the infernal theater in the East of the DRC.

Screens worldwide highlighted a stark contrast: jets shuttling leaders to meetings in luxurious offices, men and women dressed to the nines, signing peace treaties and raising glasses in the name of victims left unburied in the fields. Chin Chin! The Congo was being pulled by the highest bidder, a scene repeating itself for over 65 years. Those who missed the first shot clenched their fists and teeth, waiting for their turn, pushing to birth a new armed group. And so it went on.

When Donald Trump entered the White House, some within the Congolese diaspora saw a chance. He became the first

Western leader to impose sanctions on Rwanda's military elite. Europe, under pressure, briefly followed. But the killings did not stop.

In early 2025, the violence intensified. Millions were displaced within months. The figures grew so vast they began to lose meaning. But behind every number stood a story, a child gone missing, a mother murdered and dumped in a ditch, a baby screaming in terror beside her freshly slain body. This was not fiction. It was the brutal truth of the terrain — seen, lived, endured.

Schools turned into recruiting stations. Children were handed guns instead of pencils. Families vanished overnight. Ten million dead. Seven million displaced. Over half a million women raped. And the numbers kept climbing, creeping upward like a curse.

A handful dared to say what others glossed over. Political scientist Charles Onana, one of the rare international voices unwilling to veil the truth, titled his book *Holocaust in Congo*. He did not soften his words. He called it genocide, where the world preferred to say "conflict." He put faces to the statistics. He demanded remembrance, not mere mourning. Mourning had become a luxury denied, grief choked behind clenched teeth as entire worlds collapsed. The world watched. The world did nothing. And so, the war marched on.

In the emerald hills of Kivu, across tangled forests where gorillas still drew ragged breaths and children darted barefoot through ashes, only one question thundered through the silence: *When will it end?*

Chapter 2

The Child the Ancestors Heard

Nyota's story did not begin with her; it began with those whose bones rooted her into the earth.

Her father, Tatu, was born into the Bakwa Beya, a noble lineage anchored deep in the red soil of Kasai, where diamonds sleep just beneath the surface, awaiting the brave or the greedy. His family name carried ancestral wealth and expectations, whispered more than spoken. He was the last of twelve siblings, a wiry boy with nimble fingers and a quicker mind, born in Likasi, a copper-coated town where

Melancholy Harmonies

rust colored roads curled through scorched hills like veins carrying molten fire.

From the beginning, fate seemed to draw a circle around Tatu. Royal blood pulsed in his veins, but his heart bowed toward engines, not thrones. He had a gift for dismantling machines and putting them back together cleaner, sharper, reborn. Likasi shaped him: barefoot walks under cobalt skies, laughter drifting between rusting railcars, the blister of sun-baked asphalt against his soles. It was there, in that hum of possibility, that his path veered toward the University of Lubumbashi, and fate rewrote his story.

That was where he met Bibi.

She spoke little, but her presence commanded the room. Tall, graceful, always wrapped in crisp cotton dresses that moved like whispers, Bibi carried herself with the still power of someone who never needed to raise her voice. Her sharp, observant eyes had a way of making people sit up straighter. And her laughter? It sounded like firewood crackling at dusk — warm, steady, promising refuge.

Tatu fell at once.

She saw past his ambition, past the grease under his fingernails and the urgency in his talk. She saw him, and that was enough. By the time he earned his engineering degree in 1990, there was no hesitation left in either of them. They married quietly, binding their futures not with spectacle but with steady commitment, a shared gaze, a firm grip, and an unspoken promise to choose each other as the years rolled on.

They moved to Kolwezi, a mining town that inhaled iron dust and exhaled the roar of machinery. The air smelled of wet metal and ground-up stone. Tatu found steady work with a British corporation. They lived modestly but comfortably in a small brick house, which he lovingly renovated room by room. Their mornings were sacred —Chayi ya moto (hot teas), nkangala na mwoko, whispered jokes before sunrise, half-awake talks of the children they longed to hold.

And then came December 1993, and the rumors began. Fear does not announce itself; it creeps. Whispers circulated through Katanga, hissing warnings that no one wanted to believe. And then, without warning, the air shattered. Violence exploded. What history would later call *La Chasse aux Kasaiens* was not a hunt. A hunt implies skill, fairness, and rules. It was a massacre. The Luba people, Tatu's people, were targeted. It was ethnic cleansing disguised as nationalism. Houses burned before dawn. Families were slaughtered in the alleys, torn from under their beds. Cries mingled with smoke as Tatu fled with what mattered, Bibi and the fierce instinct to survive. The house he had built brick by brick? Reduced to ashes and memories. No one stops to save walls when the house is burning down.

They fled toward Mbuji-Mayi, hoping to blend into the dust and tumult of the diamond capital. But hope, like a house, is a fragile thing. For Tatu's surviving brothers, it had been gone for too long. He had lived among strangers, married outside their lineage, and only returned when the fire knocked at his door.

They called him "Mutoka," an outsider. And worse, Bibi was not one of them. She didn't speak the dialect fluently. She didn't bow at the expected moments. Her grace was not submission; it was strength. And that disturbed them. Still, they continued.

Tatu found work at Société Minière de Bakwanga (MIBA). Exhausting work. Long hours under metal roofs, unburned oil under his nails, steel carving furrows into his palms. It was not much, but it was something.

From this fatigue, something sacred was born, something they had awaited for five long years.

In Kasai culture, and in African culture in general, waiting that long without conceiving was not merely unfortunate; it was a scarlet letter. Gossip spread like smoke through alleyways. Women laughed behind woven fans. Men let their eyes linger just a little too long. Bibi was whispered about as *"Nkumba,"* the barren one. Not just in Tatu's household, but throughout the entire neighborhood. Her faith stayed firm, but her heart cracked quietly under the strain of each new monthly cycle, each new disappointment. Every community gathering became a test of endurance.

Melancholy Harmonies

Then, as if God had finally exhaled, Bibi's womb stirred to life.

She felt Nyota hum within her even before she missed the first cycle. The pregnancy felt like a secret miracle bubbling beneath her ribs, half joy, half disbelief. And just as her belly began to swell, another opportunity opened: IRSAC Lwiro, a research institute tucked deep in the green belly of Kivu, far from the smoke and suspicion of Mbuji-Mayi. It offered more than employment. It offered peace. Tatu accepted without blinking.

They packed their meager belongings, made silent farewells to dreams that had never sprouted roots in Mbuji Mayi, and left.

Lwiro was a world apart. The air smelled of damp bark and wildflowers. Rain fell softly, like music hummed through a veil. The villagers didn't treat them as outsiders; they welcomed them as neighbors. Tatu worked as a mechanic at the research center. Machines made sense to him. They obeyed. For once, life did too.

Nyota arrived on September 15, 2000, beneath a sky so still it felt like a long-held breath finally released. She was born at Katana Hospital, a small clinic tucked inside the IRSAC compound, surrounded more by microscopes and test tubes than bassinets and rattles. Outside, rumors whispered through the markets: rebels were coming, but when, no one knew. Anxiety hummed under every greeting, every prayer. But inside that modest delivery room, life refused to wait.

Nyota entered the world with a cry that stunned even the nurses, sharp and guttural, as though it came from someplace ancient. Tatu had prepared obsessively for her arrival: a hand-built crib, walls painted a soft yellow, roof patched twice just in case a storm thundered through. She was his daughter. His legacy. His redemption. And he would not allow war to contaminate her welcome.

As the sun dipped behind the hills, the drums began. Their throbbing echoed across the valleys, summoning aunties and cousins, neighbors and friends from distant towns. Tatu's sisters traveled for days to be there, some from Mbuji-Mayi, others from Kananga, cradling gifts wrapped in waxed fabric, hands eager to touch the miracle child.

His brothers did not come. Their absence said more than words ever could. Resentment runs deep in blood. It sat heavy in the room, as unwelcome and certain as humidity.

Still, the celebration swelled like a brewing storm. Luba women danced with regal defiance, hips swaying in rhythm to ancestral pride. Their chants rose and dipped like bone-carried stories passed from one generation to the next. A friendly rivalry broke out between the Shi chant *"O mwana akwira"* and the pulsing *"Mutwashi"* rhythm of Kasai, each daring the other to dance harder.

The air filled with the fragrant smoke of spiced meat grilling over open flames. Cassava, grilled tilapia, fried rice, and *nkalanga* were piled onto heavy plates. Beer bottles clinked, some imported from Europe, others brimming with thick, bubbling *kasikisi*, a local brew that burned like firewood going down, but lingered sweet as memory.

Inside, Bibi sat very still, watching in silence, her body still aching from the delivery. Her mind floated between joy and worry. Sitting near the cradle, she absentmindedly traced circles with the tips of her fingers on the smooth wood of the cradle. Nyota was sleeping under a light mosquito net, her tiny chest rising and falling as lantern light flickered blessings across her cheeks.

An elderly midwife stood silently near the doorway, her back curved like the crescent moon, her skin dark and polished from decades of toil. She had brought hundreds of babies into the world. None like this. Leaning forward, she whispered, "This child carries something beyond this life. A power. A destiny not written by ordinary hands."

Bibi didn't answer. As a born-again Christian, she was taught to trust scripture over signs. Yet as a daughter of Congo, she knew some truths wore no names. She did not accept the midwife's words, nor did she dismiss them. She simply whispered a prayer aimed straight for heaven.

But soon she began to understand.

Nyota did not cry like other infants. Her cries came from somewhere deeper, feral, ancient. They were not wails of hunger or discomfort, but of memory. Something unsettled. Once she began, no one could soothe her, not Tatu, not Bibi, not even the midwife whose hands had caught her from the womb. Night after night, the house echoed with her voice. The sound made the walls seem thinner; the forest leaned inward.

They took her to the clinic. The doctors measured, palpated, and listened. Their verdict was simple: "She is in good health." But Bibi knew better. Nyota was not an ordinary child. She was born of war and adoration; of heritage and prophecy. She carried a weight that no one could name. And only time would reveal what it was.

And in time, the atmosphere shifted, less singing and more terror.

The Night the Boots Turned Back

The escape began on a night darker than any Bibi had ever known, a night when it seemed even the heavens were weeping. Lightning tore the sky to ribbons, followed by the crackle of rebel gunfire. Bullets hissed through the air like spirits enraged. Cries of war echoed across the land, growing louder, feeding the fear coiled in Bibi's stomach.

Yet on that mysterious, fateful night, Princess Nyota did not cry.

Wrapped snugly against her mother's back, the ten-month-old child remained silent — her small body warm despite the icy rain seeping through the cracks of their wooden home. Bibi crouched low, resting on her knees, listening with every fibre of her being.

Tatu stood by the door, gripping a heavy wooden kitchen pestle nearly a metre long. His fingers tensed around it, knuckles white. The rebels were close. Their machetes clanged against their belts as they approached the house. Their boots, soaked with mud and rain, squelched heavily against the earth. Tatu did not lock the door. He left it slightly ajar, allowing the night to spill in. If they forced their way inside, he would be ready.

The moment struck like a thunderclap.

A single kick sent the door crashing inward. Shadows rushed into the house, their shapes merging with the darkness. The first invader roared, brandished his weapon, and stepped across the threshold.

And then, Nyota moved.

The child unleashed a sound no baby should make. It was raw. Primal. As if something ancient had awakened inside her, something boundless, enraged. The silence of the little house shattered as she leapt from Bibi's back. Barely clothed in a cotton undergarment, she soared through the air like a being unchained from the earth.

The house erupted.

Nyota snatched a spoon from the table and hurled it with unnatural precision. It struck the invading rebel in the centre of his forehead. He staggered, his breath ripped from his throat, then his body froze. His rifle slipped from his hands. His limbs locked. A strangled groan escaped him as he toppled, stone-stiff, blocking the doorway.

The second intruder had no time to react. He tripped over his fallen comrade, lurching forward, only to gasp as something invisible seized him. His throat clenched. His scream became a desperate gurgle. His eyes bulged, as if unseen hands were crushing the life out of him. Slowly, unnaturally, his body lifted an inch from the ground, just long enough for the terror to register.

A third rebel tried to flee. He lurched backward, banging into the others, forcing their way through the doorway, their war cries twisting into yelps of confusion and raw horror.

The very air inside the house began to distort.

The walls seemed to pulse, shadows skittering in unnatural patterns. A furious, unseen presence swirled in the room like a gathering storm. Outside, the wind shrieked, slamming rain against the frail wooden structure as if it were alive. Inside, the air thickened; a suffocating pressure squeezed every chest, making even breathing feel dangerous.

And then the house inhaled.

A violent gust exploded from the centre of the room, a cyclone unbound. The rebels were sucked into the spiraling wind, their screams devoured by the deafening roar. The tiny home became the eye of a tempest, a tornado born from nowhere, hurling bodies against walls, against each other, tearing weapons from their grasp. They spun like rag dolls, helpless against the invisible force.

All the while, Tatu watched, frozen and disbelieving, the pestle sliding unnoticed from his fingers. It wasn't the wind that terrified him. It was the feeling, something ancient and wild crawling up his spine. He felt it in his bones, in his gut. He knew, without knowing how he knew, it was coming from her.

From Nyota.

She hovered mid-air, a baby no longer but a force. Tiny fists clenched. Eyes glowing with a dark, otherworldly light. Deep pools of midnight fixed on the intruders. Nyota did not look human in that moment. She looked ancient.

Bibi and Tatu stood paralysed, their minds failing to grasp the impossible scene before them. Perhaps they were dreaming. Perhaps this was death. Each silently wished for someone to pinch them, anything to prove they were still alive.

Then, as abruptly as it had begun, the chaos ceased.

The rebels lay sprawled on the ground, motionless. Silence descended, heavy and loaded, broken only by the distant howl of wind outside.

Tatu's breath came fast and shallow. He turned slowly toward Bibi, sweat breaking anew across his brow.

"We have to go," he whispered. Then, more urgently, "Now. We cross the lake. We head for the Rwandan border."

Bibi nodded, clutching Nyota, once more quietly strapped to her back, soft and serene, as if she had never moved at all.

Tatu pushed forward, leading them out the back of the house. Their feet pounded against the waterlogged earth. The fence circling their yard, brittle with age and rot, splintered as they crashed through it, racing toward the shadowy outline of Lake Kivu.

The night stretched ahead of them, vast, uncertain, dangerous.

The main gate of the compound was blocked by the body of Mata, their faithful guard. His corpse floated in a dark pool of blood, eyes wide, reflecting the flickering fires devouring distant homes. There was no time for grief, no time for prayer, only movement.

"Is she asleep?" Bibi asked for the first time since they had begun to run, turning so Tatu could see Nyota's tiny head.

"She's resting," Tatu murmured, though he did not truly look.

He grabbed Bibi's hand, pulling her onward. Nyota, once wild and fearsome, now lay strangely peaceful, as if guarding her strength for whatever came next.

They could not stop. They could not look back. Behind them, the impossible had just happened. Ahead of them, whatever lay waiting would never be the same.

They plunged into the jungle, a living maze of ancient trees, twisted roots, and whispering shadows. The path they followed was known only to those who had lived here long enough to understand its secrets: rare snakes glided silently beneath fallen leaves, unseen gorillas watched from deeper darkness. Yet none interfered. It was as if the forest itself parted for them, granting passage on this night of terror.

Tatu led, machete glinting in moonlight as he sliced vines and thick brush. Every rustle made their hearts stumble. Bibi nearly fell on a gnarled root, suppressing a cry; Tatu caught her arm, steadying her before pressing on. They trampled over serpents without receiving a single bite. No gorilla crossed their path. It was as though the jungle protected them, or feared what walked behind them.

After countless miles and five ghostlike villages, where terrified faces peered from shattered doors, they reached the black, endless sweep of Lake Kivu.

A man stepped from the shadows.

Safari.

Safari. His name derives its full meaning from the service he provides to the Wasafiri, the travelers, in Swahili. He offers this service not without a heavy heart, aiding fugitives who have abandoned their villages with little hope of ever seeing them again. According to some beliefs, Safari embodies the ancestors, ensuring that the land is not emptied and that the few who remain multiply like ants, to avenge and preserve the sacred, coveted lands.

His name was spoken only in whispers, the kind of whisper used by people who had survived. He ferried souls across the water, away from war, into whatever safety lay beyond.

Melancholy Harmonies

"I've prepared a raft," he said quickly, gesturing to a small inflatable craft bobbing in the shallows.

They hurried toward it, but as they drew close, it was clear: the raft was far too small. Bibi and Nyota could not possibly fit together.

"There's another boat," Safari said, his voice grave. He guided them toward an old wooden canoe patched so many times it looked more like hope than a vessel. It floated in the shallows, leaking and battered, but it was all they had.

Gunfire cracked again in the distance. Louder. Closer.

Tatu didn't hesitate. He lifted Bibi and Nyota into the canoe and climbed in after them, seizing an oar with both hands. The moment they pushed off, the lake swallowed them in icy silence.

Tatu rowed with every scrap of strength left in his body. Water slapped the cracked wood, seeping through gaps and splinters. He prayed it would hold together. Bibi gagged at the stench — bodies floated on the surface, mouths frozen in screams, eyes glassy with anguish. Some had clearly been tortured. Others simply left to drown. Death lay over the lake like a second skin.

Still, they pressed on.

But the lake had its own will.

A brutal wind rose from the east, sudden and wild, lashing the water into jagged waves. Thunder cracked overhead. Rain whipped their faces. The canoe rocked violently. Tatu gritted his teeth, digging the oar into the water with burning arms. Beside him, Bibi sobbed softly, pressing her lips to Nyota's forehead and whispering prayers snatched away by the storm.

Tatu let out a cry, forced it into a grunt of effort, and said to his wife, "Take care of the child." He meant focus and courage. Bibi heard a farewell.

Then came a sound. A low, guttural rumble, inhuman, responding from somewhere across the water. The air shifted.

Melancholy Harmonies

The storm struck like a living thing, a vortex of wind and water spiraling down upon them with fury beyond nature. The canoe pitched. Water boiled beneath them, as if unseen hands were trying to drag them under. Waves rose like liquid mountains.

Nyota, strapped to her back, faced Bibi's chest, clinging tightly to her wrap against the wind, the tides, the liquid hills. Bibi bowed her head over her daughter, pressing her lips to the small forehead. Her back became a shield against the storm, against the threat bearing down on what she cherished most in the world, this child who had just committed the unthinkable in their household, leaving a bloodbath behind.

The canoe nearly capsized. It was not an ordinary storm. It was... something else.

And then, silence.

The lake stilled. The wind died. The water went eerily smooth and calm, as if it had never moved at all. Tatu gasped for breath, muscles trembling from exhaustion. Bibi stared first at Nyota and then at the darkness around them, eyes wide and haunted. There was no explanation.

Eventually, Nyota tucked her head under Bibi's chin, peaceful as a lamb. Bibi fed her carefully from a small jar of cow's milk, hands still shaking.

Tatu rowed on past pain, past terror, driven only by sheer will. Hours passed until at last a thin line of gold crept over the horizon.

Land.

Cyangugu, Rwanda. White UN buses waited on the shore like ghosts from another world. The canoe scraped the bank. Tatu collapsed over the side, panting. Bibi stepped out gently with Nyota in her arms.

They had survived.

A UN worker appeared, waving them toward a bus bound for the Nyamasheke refugee camp.

Tatu touched Nyota's hand. "We made it," he whispered.

Bibi nodded, but her eyes were still distant and dark.

They had escaped the war, but the ghosts of that night would follow them forever.

Chapter 4

The Country Where Nothing Is Free

The road to the camp was a long ribbon of red dust, snaking through Rwandan hills dotted with eucalyptus and banana trees. The heat pressed down relentlessly, the sun beating against the roof of the taxi like a drum. Inside, Princess Nyota slept quietly against Bibi's chest, lulled by the engine's hum. Tatu stared through the dusty window, watching barefoot children chasing chickens between mud-brick houses, their laughter rising above a silence thick with things unspoken.

"I'm not staying here," Tatu said suddenly, his voice firm with decision. "I have a brother in America. He will take us in."

Bibi did not protest. She simply held their daughter tighter.

At the registration center, a caseworker listened as Tatu explained that his older brother, Kabunji, had been living in New York for years. He had escaped another war long ago. He would help them. The caseworker nodded slowly. It was rare for refugees to leave so soon, but families with confirmed sponsors abroad occasionally bypassed the endless waiting of camp life.

Tatu moved quickly, refusing to waste a single hour. He spent every moment filling out forms, chasing signatures, nudging the labyrinth of bureaucracy forward with pure determination.

The site teemed with people seeking exile: bewildered men, mothers holding feverish children, young people with broken looks. In the corridors, people alternated between speaking French, English, and Swahili.

A few "hello," "hi," and diplomatic smiles circulated among the agents, contrasting sharply with the cruel weariness etched on the applicants' faces.

Tatu observed everything silently. He joined a small group of Congolese in the midst of a heated dispute.

"Who goes first?" asked one.

"It's not a matter of who goes first," grumbled another, his features drawn. "I've been here for four days. Others arrived yesterday, and they've already been called!"

They spoke of discreet corruption, favouritism, and unequal chances. One father wanted to emigrate to Belgium, believing the former colonisers owed something in return.

He had no one to welcome him, his application was blocked, and he had been sleeping on the spot for days. "The Belgians colonised us and plundered our resources," he said aloud, as if to provoke discussion. "I've been here for over four days. People who came after me are already being served, and I'm still waiting," he added, leaning on a wooden frame. "You can at least have mercy on my poor family, whom I haven't seen in a long time."

"Calm down, Mzee, everyone will be served sooner or later."

"I know that, but I no longer want to hear the word 'later.'"

The immigration requirements for this father and his family had not been met, which was why he lingered here. Apart from him, a few other families had literally made this place their home. Every weekend, a vehicle would come to pick up those who had been sleeping here for days and take them away.

This phrase, *"I no longer want to hear the word late,"* struck Tatu with full force. He understood that nothing would be simple, that waiting could break men as surely as war. Accessing the United Nations High Commissioner for Refugees (UNHCR) was difficult, and the agents were overwhelmed by the sheer volume of requests. Still, it must be recalled that compared to the number of displaced persons, those who gathered here were only a small fraction, less than five percent, of those crying out in the camps where the humanitarian situation remained alarming and incredibly miserable despite several campaigns.

Tatu listened to the discussion without saying a word. He was speechless. The more hours passed, the more hope diminished. Since the morning, they had only served three people! Rumors circulated in the corridors that these individuals had used their connections in Rwanda to influence the UNHCR agents. Tatu was exhausted, worn out.

He returned to the displaced persons' site, weighed down by sorrow, as the night dragged on endlessly. Between Nyota's moans and Bibi's silence, he had more regrets than dreams, which he tried to envision despite everything. The village he left behind was in dust and the ashes of the dead. He felt like he was chasing the wind endlessly. He could never have imagined himself in this situation.

That evening, he returned to the tarpaulin tent at the displaced persons' site, his throat tight. Nyota moaned in her sleep; Bibi remained silent, looking away. Tatu stepped outside to get fresh air. It was midnight, and he could not sleep. He let himself go into meditation. In front of him, the camp stretched as far as the eye could see. The fluttering of insect wings and a few whistles from nocturnal birds intermittently broke the silence. A few dogs barked in the distance. The stars, shy behind heavy clouds, seemed to mock his meager hopes for better tomorrows.

He almost cried out, then sobbed quietly. Fearing he would wake Nyota and panic Bibi, he pulled himself together, swallowing hard, his jaws clenched, the lump in his throat, quickly wiping away a few tears. The scene of this gloomy night worsened his mood. He then decided to go back to the small room. Before entering, he tested the sturdiness of the roof sheltering them with his hand and shook his head in bitter frustration.

The next day, he went back to the UNHCR. Same setting, same faces, though new arrivals had been added, their beards not yet grown long. But still the same growling and head-shaking signs of despair. Until an employee approached Bibi, moved by the sight of her breastfeeding the exhausted Nyota. Out of compassion, she decided to expedite their case, which was actually not complicated. They had just escaped imminent death.

By the second sunrise, they were squeezed into the back of a rusty taxi, hurtling toward Kigali Airport.

The driver flew around sharp mountain bends as though chasing death itself, skirting cliffs where a single miscalculation would send them tumbling into ravines below.

"Yesterday, a whole family went over the edge," he said casually, barely glancing at the road.

Tatu snapped, "Shut up! You want to kill us too?"

Melancholy Harmonies

Bibi closed her eyes, clutching Nyota so tightly that she could feel her own heart pounding through her chest.

He's a sorcerer, and he wants to sacrifice us, she thought silently and prayed loudly.

He began a dizzying, winding descent between the hills before reaching a long, straight stretch, and finally slowed. Bibi bit back a cry, clutching Nyota tighter as the taxi swerved. The driver only laughed, slowing only when the road straightened, leading them onto a long, flat stretch of tarmac.

"Almost there," he announced. "The danger is over!"

Tatu wasn't convinced. His palms were slick with sweat; he rubbed them along his jeans, trying to settle his racing heart, but relief refused to come.

They spent one last night in Rwanda, tucked inside a small hotel near the airport, a place known for housing refugee families in transit to faraway countries they had only ever seen on television. Sleep did not come. Tatu lay awake thinking about everything they had endured and everything he could not predict. Bibi remained silent beside him, eyes open in the dark.

Before dawn, another taxi delivered them to the departure terminal. The line of refugees stretched endlessly, a trembling river of people gripping suitcases, bundles, and babies. Children clutched their mothers' skirts as if afraid they might be left behind.

Tatu muttered under his breath as they stepped forward inch by inch, "All this… it's too organized. Someone is forcing these people to flee their own lands."

Bibi said nothing. There was nothing left to say.

The flight to America was announced, and they crossed through the gate, into a future both terrifying and unknown.

***

The ten-hour flight from Kigali to New York felt longer than any journey Tatu or Bibi had ever taken. The plane hummed with soft conversations and the clatter of meal trays, but nothing brought them comfort. Nyota refused rest, squirming in Bibi's arms, turning away from breast milk, everything. It was only when Tatu pressed her against his chest, rocking gently, that she finally fell into an uneasy sleep.

When the wheels touched the runway at John F. Kennedy International Airport (JFK), there was a ripple of applause, a ritual of nervous travelers grateful to have made it. But to Tatu, the sound was hollow, almost eerie. His heart did not lift. Instead, a heavy knot of uncertainty grew as he watched unfamiliar lights streak past the window.

At the nearly empty arrivals hall, a short, stocky man paced in front of a vending machine. Kabunji, Tatu's big brother. His belly stretched a faded hoodie, and his skinny legs were squeezed into jeans that seemed too young for him. The moment he spotted them, he stopped pacing but did not smile.

"Follow me," he barked. "I don't have much time. I work tomorrow morning."

No hugs. No welcome.

Tatu's face tightened with disappointment. "This is how you greet me after all these years? No embrace? No joy?" he said as they hurried to keep up with Kabunji's brisk pace. "If it weren't for your voice, I wouldn't even recognize you. What happened, brother? Too many American hamburgers?"

"Let's go, please," Bibi said to her husband.

Melancholy Harmonies

She was less worried about her brother-in-law's mood. In Congo, she had learned that black people living in Europe and America also chased after time. She prayed that her husband would understand Kabunji as quickly as possible and not disturb him. Despite herself, she adapted to the pace.

Kabunji ignored his brother's remark, weaving through elevators, endless corridors, and moving walkways. Without warning, they found themselves outside, in the fresh air, in front of the bus stop. Bibi had taken the precaution of checking the climate. She had brought all the warm clothes offered by the agents during their stay in Kigali.

After about ten minutes, the bus arrived. Inside the bus, the city flashed past the windows; the tall buildings cast shadows on the streets below. Tatu perceived only a vague glow of lights, which he compared to the darkness left behind. He was lost in thought. Was he really in the land of dreams, America, the land of opportunity, and Uncle Sam's country?

A heaviness weighed on his chest as these questions hammered in his mind. He whispered to himself, *"So this is America. It's going to be fine,"* repeating the words for courage. But what he was about to experience would shatter his fragile hope.

An hour later, the bus stopped on a narrow street. Kabunji threw his hands theatrically toward a glowing yellow sign.

"Welcome to America! Look, McDonald's! Let's eat."

Tatu remained speechless for a long moment and let out, without pretending: "A fast food restaurant?"

Kabunji was already in line inside, signaling them to move toward an empty table. They hesitated, but followed. Bibi dragged her feet before collapsing onto a chair with her child in her arms. Their bodies screamed for rest! They collapsed in exhaustion around a plate of fries.

While they were eating, Kabunji rummaged through his black backpack and pulled out a black plastic canister. Without saying a word, he headed toward a fountain and activated it with his hand.

Tatu looked at him, eyebrows furrowed, mouth slightly open, "What are you doing?"

"I'm collecting free drinks," replied Kabunji in a neutral tone. Then he added, "Here, we don't waste anything. This will be your drink for the week. In America, there are plenty of 'free deals,' food offers like two for one, discount coupons. I collect everything so I don't spend too much.

"Wow!" Tatu exclaimed, surprised, uttering this expression for the first time. He had learned it from a French movie. Tatu rubbed his temples. This was not the dream he had pictured.

Bibi's eyelids were closed, and she struggled to lift her head to see what was happening.

When the meal was done, they walked fifteen painful minutes to Kabunji's apartment, a cramped two-room dwelling that smelled of cheap paint and colder hopes. A sofa-bed faced a tiny kitchenette, and a toilet stood in plain view. Up a narrow staircase was a loft smaller than a storage closet.

Bibi sank wordlessly onto the couch, pulling Nyota beneath a thin, musty blanket. Silence hung in the room; no one spoke.

***

Morning crashed in without warning. The door burst open, and Kabunji stepped in, followed by a tall, bearded stranger.

"What are you still doing here?" Kabunji barked. "This is my roommate's space!"

Tatu shot to his feet, anger flooding through his exhaustion. "You dumped us here without telling us where to sleep. After everything we've been through, not even instructions?"

Voices rose sharply. Hands clenched. At last, Tatu made a decision.

"We're leaving."

Bibi clutched Nyota and followed him out into the cold street. Behind them, Kabunji shouted, "I told you, in America, nothing is free!"

"Yes, you must give the money you brought!" the bearded stranger added.

Bibi choked back a sob. Nyota was whimpering softly. Where could they go now?

The words stung, but they did not turn back.

They wandered aimlessly, homeless in a city of millions. Nyota whimpered against her mother's chest. Bibi sniffled quietly. Then, as if God himself intervened, a yellow cab slowed beside them. The driver leaned out, worry creasing his brow.

"How may I help you?"

Tatu's English was broken, desperate. "No place. No food. No sleep. Baby. We are from Africa."

The driver nodded and motioned them inside.

Minutes later, they arrived at a building marked "Refugee Center." The driver did not abandon them; he walked them in and explained to the receptionist. Warmth met them for the first time since stepping off the plane.

Three weeks passed. Paperwork. Checks. A cot in a shared room. Then the letter arrived: authorization to work.

A friend offered Tatu a drive into the city. But when Nyota was strapped into a car seat for the first time, she howled, fists pounding, eyes wild. Startled, Bibi unbuckled her immediately and held her close.

At a stop sign, a police officer appeared. Their driver explained, "They are new, from Africa. She doesn't like the car seat."

The officer watched Nyota wailing in her mother's arms and waved them on.

At home, the irony struck them: Nyota refused to sleep unless she was in someone's arms, or in the car seat she had once rejected. The crib remained untouched.

Concerned, Bibi took her to a nearby clinic, where a Nigerian midwife smiled softly after examination.

"Your daughter is perfectly healthy," she said. "She simply has a 'great destiny.'"

The paediatrician cautioned them about co-sleeping, listing risks and statistics. But Bibi knew her daughter better than statistics.

Nyota grew quickly, bright-eyed, and strangely composed.

At four years old, she stood fearless before a crowd of three hundred in church and spoke with such confidence that grown men leaned forward to listen.

Some mothers whispered that she was unnerving, that in their tradition, a child should lower their gaze before elders. But American teachers praised her poise.

Nyota wasn't just different. She was born for something greater.

She was called.

Chapter 5

The Song That Drew the Wolf

Christmas 2005 arrived like a storm of lights, and American customs were still difficult for Bibi to understand. The streets buzzed with activity. Christian or not, all religions combined, in the United States, Christmas is Christmas.

Bibi remembered her first Christmas with nostalgia and melody, back in 2001, when her family was still searching for each other in New York. Everything was centered around gifts. Everywhere she went, and with everyone she spoke to, it was always: "Are you ready for Christmas? Did you buy gifts?"

She would quickly respond, "Yeah," and avoid the conversation because her English was limited.

The Americans didn't seem to mind her accent; on the contrary, she often heard them say, "Oh, I like your accent. Where are you from?"

"Sorry, I need to use the restroom," she would say as she escaped to the nearest public restroom. Tatu, completely unrestrained, always teased her about her quick escapes to the bathrooms. Tatu would speak to her with big hand and foot gestures, making Bibi laugh uncontrollably until tears streamed down her face.

"You're doing Mangobo here with these Americans," she would often say, imitating Tatu's funny gestures.

Americans, men and women alike, were simply being friendly. It happened everywhere, in public places and in store lines.

The Christmas atmosphere always brought back those memories for Bibi: her very first Christmas in the United States, an electric and frenzied vibe where people hurried around with a list in hand to buy gifts. No one wanted to forget a name. They'd never been used to this tradition of exchanging presents.

"But if we have to exchange gifts, what's the point?" protested Tatu, almost embarrassed by the culture. "Just keep your gift, and I'll keep mine. That's all."

Bibi rolled her eyes and said, "That's true, but you also have to be careful: the two exchanged gifts should be of equal value.

"What?!"

"Yeah, otherwise someone feels ripped off!"

"I've never been into that gift-giving thing; it's for women."

Melancholy Harmonies

"But it's nice, though. You have to respect it and especially honor the protocol. Christmas here means decorations on the streets, in public squares, in stores, hospitals, and even prisons. Christmas kicks off with Santa, dressed up near a shop, holding a basket of donations. He jingles his bell at the sight of every person. Stores smell of cinnamon, vanilla, and lavender. Huge Christmas trees decorate every corner, in shops, at the hospital, and outside homes. Spectacular lights blink in green, red, and white. Christmas carols echo through loudspeakers, in cars, even at gas stations. Malls are packed with impatient shoppers scurrying toward the checkout, eyes nervously checking their watches. The salespeople, standing for hours, greet every customer leaving with a "Thank you for coming," accompanied by a forced smile. And then one: "Next, please."

"At least in the U.S., customer service is respectful," Bibi said while shopping. "My friend in Belgium says you cannot return or exchange an item once you have bought it."

"Oh yes, sometimes people overdo it here in the U.S., especially Africans. They buy, use, and then come back to return things to get their money back. That is not honest."

"Not in all stores. Remember that story of the young girl who tried to return her wedding dress? Even though she took care to have it cleaned at the dry cleaners, the seller detected that it had been worn. And she was ridiculous for demanding her money back. How embarrassing!"

Laughter erupted, memories of events they had experienced together on this land of hope and opportunity. Cheerful, humorous conversations filled the air beneath rustic, sparkling lights flickering on shop windows. All of this signaled a Christmas that was both sensational and moving for Tatu, his little family, and the church they attended.

Hidden Manna Church is no exception to the colorful Christmas atmosphere, despite its doctrine that emphasizes the Holy Spirit and the true meaning of Christ's birth, as well as His humble entry into the world. The afternoon service, which is supposed to last two hours, can sometimes extend to three hours depending on the spirit and prophecy. But the pastor always takes into account the family dinner, which often takes place after the service, or the well-wrapped gifts piled under a decorated and illuminated tree.

The night from December 24th to 25th is the longest for children, who eagerly await the discovery of their presents.

Some impatient little ones tear open their packages while their parents are still sleeping.

Nyota, always skeptical, doubts the existence of Santa Claus, considering him a commercial fabrication.

She often asked Bibi, "Mom, the Santa at school sounded like Mr. Jones, the man who lives next door. I saw his shoes!"

"Really, child," said Tatu. He whispered to his wife, *"Ambia mtoto kweli,"* which means, "Tell the truth to the child."

Bibi pretended not to hear anything.

Nyota hurried ahead of her parents, eager and impatient to go to church. She would be the first in line in the car, all excited. This Sunday, December 24th, 2005, the church was preparing to welcome the world. The faithful, dressed to the nines, were all in red, green, black, and white. A buzz of contagious joy filled the air.

Voices rose in cheerful greetings. "Hello, brother! Sister! Merry Christmas!" called an elderly woman, waving energetically. "You look great!" shouted a man from the back pew. "You too! Thank you!" replied the woman, her laughter mingling with the chatter around them.

The atmosphere was charged with an extraordinary presence, a prelude to an unexpected miracle. The piano carried the music through the room, weaving into the hum of voices and soft prayers. Suddenly, a piercing cry echoed; heads turned toward the noise, then quickly returned to their reverence, prayers, and folded hands. Nothing serious, just a woman who had fainted in ecstasy while moving her lips. She was already surrounded by two elderly women in uniform, ready to support her with draped fabrics behind her.

The temple was full, a huge shimmering pine tree stood near the altar. Nyota was walking in front of her parents, her gaze fixed on a painted dove above the pulpit, a symbol of the Holy Spirit.

In the middle of the service, the children's choir took their places. Their voices swelled. "My Beloved is the most beautiful," they sang in unison. The chorus of "Yeshoua" grew louder, and some worshipers broke down in tears.

Then, unprompted, Nyota stepped forward. She moved down the aisle and gently took the microphone from the teenage choir leader. The pianist, surprised, gave a discreet nod and changed the key.

Melancholy Harmonies

The congregation held its breath, eyes exchanging glances, fixed on this small, graceful being in motion. She had been sent out there, in front. And then, her voice filled the room: "Yours is the kingdom, Yours is the power, Yours is the glory, forever, amen."

The girl's voice rose, full of fire and sacred wounds. People were shouting, collapsing, and hitting the ground on their knees. The pastor remained standing, mouth open, Bible suspended between his fingers. It was as if the sky had descended into the room. The gentle melody, the atmosphere of worship and prayer combined—it was as if the service was led by angels themselves.

Nyota, in tears, fell to her knees without stopping her song. When she finished, the children of the choir surrounded her with admiration. She returned to her parents amid a moving ovation. Bibi showered her with kisses, while Tatu gently wiped her eyes. Pastor Smith Anderson then stepped forward purposefully to the pulpit.

"Praise the Lord," he said solemnly.

"Hallelujah," responded the congregation.

"Merry Christmas," he said again with a big smile. Then, he silenced the faithful's ovations and continued, his gaze fixed on his Bible: Matthew 19:13–14: *"Then children were brought to him so that he might lay his hands on them and pray. But the disciples rebuked them. Jesus said, 'Let the little children come to me, and do not hinder them, for the kingdom of heaven belongs to such as these.'"*

You could hear a fly buzz. After a few seconds, only the sound of the wind could be heard, followed by the hum of a car whose noise faded away along a road lined with trees.

Then the pastor called out, "Let us hear an Amen!" The congregation responded, followed by a "Praise the Lord" and a resounding "Hallelujah," reviving the room that had been immersed in silence. Pastor Anderson scanned the entire assembly with a paternal gaze.

"Beloved brothers and sisters," he resumed with renewed strength, "it is curious to note that it is the disciples who pushed away the children brought to Jesus. And that's often what we, who believe we have the merit of following the Lord, do as well.

Why don't we give them the opportunity to serve their Master? Why don't we take the time to discover them? To know their hidden gifts? Instead of leaving them prey to the dangers lurking on the internet? These children need our presence in their lives, not gifts to fill a void created by our absence."

No response.

"Today, we wanted to dedicate this day to children, to let them teach us something, in one way or another. Let's imagine, for a moment, that someone prevented this little girl, whose heart was boiling for the Lord, from singing. We would have missed the most beautiful moment of this service."

"Yes, yes!" cried someone from the crowd.

Others quickly followed, echoing the response.

"I love you, baby," Bibi whispered into her daughter's ear. She was electrified with joy.

"You ask how these little ones bring down God's presence?" the pastor asked. "The answer is before your eyes, in verse 1 of Matthew, chapter 19."

"The kingdom of heaven belongs to such as these," he said, *"and to those who become like them.* If we want to inherit the kingdom of heaven, we must become like these children; they do not worry because they are sure that their parents will take care of them. How many times do we fall into anxiety and stress, which bring us nothing? Trust in God, and He will take care of you."

"I will not take much of your time," the pastor said as he closed his Bible. His eyes scanned the room. "I do not doubt that you have thought of your children present here. But let us also think of those who are far away, living in misery and war. Those abandoned on the streets, living in inhumane conditions, and those who are victims of abuse and harassment, bearing wounds in their hearts that still bleed.

They feel contaminated, watching a society indifferent to their lives and their innocence."

"I leave you with this question: On the eve of Christmas, who will be that person, in the image of Jesus, who will say, *'Let the little children come to me.'* To care for them, help them, listen to them?"

"May the Lord bless you!"

"Amen," the faithful responded in unison, rising from their benches and moving toward the church exit.

Throughout the evening, messages flooded Tatu and Bibi's phones: "Take care of this child." "She is not ordinary." "Protect her destiny."

Words they had heard before.

Later, during the Christmas meal, Nyota suddenly lifted her head, just as she had when she was two, and said in a calm, confident tone, "I saw us in a bigger house... a gate, a garden, and angels guarding it."

Tatu burst out laughing, deeply moved. "We will need a big house to keep our little angel."

Bibi shivered.

She knew, this time without a doubt, that their daughter did not belong to the ordinary world.

From the very beginning, Nyota was different.

At just two years old, she was often found sitting on the living room rug, a broken toy guitar across her knees, plucking its plastic strings as seriously as a conductor, as if, through the power of her imagination, she could make real notes emerge.

One day, while Bibi folded laundry, the child stopped abruptly, looked up with serious eyes, and said in a calm, assured voice, "I saw that we lived in a big house. It was beautiful. We all lived together."

A cold shiver ran down Bibi's spine. At that time, the family was still crammed into Kabunji's apartment, too small and filled with noise, fatigue, and overcrowding. The idea of a big house seemed absurd then, almost ridiculous. Tatu burst out laughing, brushing it off as a child's fantasy. But Nyota watched them intently, steady as a witness, her burning eyes holding a truth only she understood.

Melancholy Harmonies

Two years later, however, they stood at the threshold of a new home, somewhere in a quiet American suburb: manicured lawn, quietness, newness, peaceful light filtering through huge windows. It was no mansion, but for them it was a palace. Bibi spent the first night unable to sleep, her heart struck by a certainty: their daughter was seeing, not imagining.

From that day on, they learned to see her differently. Nyota was not growing; she was radiating. Long before she could write her name, she was already composing melodies. She hummed alone for hours, drumming on tables, windowsills, handles, transforming every object into an instrument. It wasn't a game; it was a call.

Tatu, moved by pride and worry alike, saved penny by penny from his warehouse worker's salary to fill the house with small instruments: tambourines, toy keyboards, mini drums, and for her fifth birthday, a real guitar, too expensive for their budget but impossible to refuse. From then on, silence became a distant memory. Even at night, Nyota moved her foot under the blanket, like an internal metronome refusing to sleep.

At school, she often kept to herself, sitting under a tree with a notebook on her knees, blackening pages filled with words intertwined with drawings. By the age of six, she was already writing complete stories, accompanied by hums, as if each sentence had to be born in music. She would ask her mother to mimic certain sounds, just "to hear a rhythm again."

One afternoon, she burst into the apartment, breathless, still dressed in her school uniform.

"Mama! Baba!" she exclaimed, cheeks flushed. "Near my school, there's a singing teacher who gives lessons to children. It's not expensive. I want to learn for real!"

Bibi and Tatu exchanged a glance. There was a determination in that little head far greater than her size.

Bibi cupped her cheek. "Are you sure?"

Nyota nodded so hard her braids bounced.

"All right," Tatu said. "We'll sign you up."

And so, without realizing it, they opened the door to Nyota's next step, the one that would change everything, for better and for worse.

The first lessons seemed harmless. Once a week, after school, Nyota went to see Mr. Sims, an old music teacher with a round belly, white hair, and a grandfatherly smile. The living room was covered with a plush brown rug. The children practiced on one side, while the parents sat on metal chairs, watching from afar. His wife, a gentle and discreet Korean woman, moved around them with fruit juices and cookies, repeating: "Don't worry, parents, we're taking good care of your little ones."

Trust grew quickly, like a weed. Soon, the parents began taking advantage of the lessons to do some shopping, leaving their children in the couple's care. As enrollments increased,

Sims moved the group upstairs, into a larger room, accessed through a small wooden door.

"Better acoustics," he said.

Downstairs, the parents chit-chatted. Upstairs, away from prying eyes, something else was happening.

Nyota was six when she started. Sims was immediately effusive. "A rare talent," he murmured, casting a moist gaze upon her that Bibi took for admiration. "I want to give her special attention."

They thought they heard Blessing, but they were mistaken.

He started to keep her "a little longer" after the other students had left, claiming it was for a special rehearsal before the concerts. Flattered, Bibi agreed.

One day, arriving earlier than expected, she entered to find Nyota kneeling near the piano, Sims standing much too close.

She leaned over him like an animal ready to pounce. Startled, he straightened up, wearing a wide, sweet smile. Bibi felt something twist inside her, a dark premonition, which she immediately dismissed out of fear of overreacting.

The trap was already closing.

Everything fell into darkness on the first night.

He had left Nyota alone while everyone else had gone, claiming it was to have her repeat her scale one last time. Without warning, the lights went out. Then they flickered back on, dimmer. Sims wandered around the room, muttering. Nyota held her guitar, tense.

He whispered that he had a Christmas gift for her and ordered her to close her eyes. When she opened them, he had exposed himself.

Her heart pounded like a war drum.

Without saying a word, he took her small hand, not in play, but in a way that made her recoil. "Touch me... make me feel good. Haven't I been good to you? Gave you toys, special snacks, Christmas gifts? You're my smart girl."

He forced her hand to rub him through his underwear while she trembled, dizzy with fear. "Good girl," he whispered, then let her leave with a small stuffed toy. "Don't tell anyone. Your parents will be angry. This is our secret, and it'll make you wiser than them."

That was the beginning of the ritual.

It continued for months. Mr. Sims arranged it so that Nyota was always the last student left. She became terrified of the sound of the small door locking behind the others. He grew increasingly controlling, insisting she sit closer, then on his lap, running his hands up her thighs as he "adjusted her posture," breathing heavy under the pretense of guiding her voice.

He gave her trinkets, glitter pens, cheap bracelets, and tiny Christmas toys as payment.

"Didn't I buy you nice toys?" he reminded her often. "Then give me what I ask, and you'll be smart and wise."

Nyota felt nauseous each time. She stopped singing out loud and only mouthed the words. Whenever she hesitated, he repeated the threat: "If you tell your parents, they'll be furious with you. You'll be in big trouble."

She was six, afraid of everything: punishment, immigration officers, the dark, and so she protected him with her silence.

One afternoon, when she was nearly eight, Sims asked her for "something special." He locked the stairway door, dimmed the lights, and tried to push her head between his thighs. She gagged, fighting him, choking on bile. He turned the stereo up loud so no one would hear.

Every week, he asked for "small favors": "Touch me again." "Rub harder." "Don't be afraid, this is your new toy."

Nyota, terrified and confused, obeyed. She vomited once after a session; he turned the music up loud so no one could hear. She washed her hands until they were raw, but never told her parents, not even when he pushed deeper into evil and demanded a sexual act she did not understand how to name. She could not find the words, not even in her own language. Fear wrapped itself around her throat like a snake.

At home, she became quieter, withdrawn. Sometimes she sang with her keyboard late at night and sobbed while she played. Tatu assumed it was just sensitivity. Bibi thought perhaps she was overwhelmed with lessons. They did not imagine the horror.

Her breaking point came unexpectedly one afternoon. As they were getting ready to leave for another lesson, she froze at the door and whispered, "Mama, I cannot go."

"Why? Are you sick?"

Chapter 6

Nyota Despised Herself

Nyota despised her body, her skin, and the bloodline that lived inside her. She felt filthy, broken, stained by a shame she could not name. Being a girl was already unbearable; being an African girl was worse. She hated the sound of her own name, the girl staring back at her in the mirror, even the family she had been born into.

But she never said a word.

At school, Princess Nyota was brilliant, energetic, and kindhearted. She had friends. She wore confidence like a second skin and dazzled in every hall she crossed.

She sang in the choir, played basketball with enviable passion, and seemed to rise effortlessly in everything she touched. From the outside, her light appeared impossible to dim. But sometimes even the brightest lights can burn out in silence.

One afternoon, she stormed through the front door in tears, cheeks hot, eyes wild, and ran straight into the living room.

"Take them out," she pleaded to her mother, nearly choking on the words. "Please, Mama… take them out!"

Bibi stared, startled, laundry still in her hands. "Take what out, my baby?"

"My braids," Nyota sobbed, clawing at the freshly done African cornrows styled just the night before. "I don't want them. I hate them!"

Bibi frowned and hurried toward her daughter.

Bibi knelt beside her, heart breaking at the sight of her usually fearless daughter unraveling.

"I'll get the aspirin spray," she said gently, eyeing the tightness of the braids and spotting small bumps swelling between the neat rows. "You must have a terrible headache. I'll spray your scalp and give you Tylenol. Then you can rest, okay?"

Nyota shook her head violently, tears streaming.

"No, Mama, that's not it! I don't want the pain to stop. I want this hair to disappear. I'm not hurting here." She tapped her head. "I'm hurting here." She pressed a fist against her chest.

"It's my heart, Mama. It feels like something's stuck in my throat and I can't breathe."

Bibi froze, a chill running through her. Something deeper was wrong. She placed a trembling hand on Nyota's shoulder, not knowing she was touching years of unspoken trauma that had never been named.

In her daughter's gaze, Bibi saw a pain that no medicine could soothe. She placed her hands on her fragile shoulders, horrified at the thought that something she had done with love, those carefully arranged braids from the day before, could become a source of shame.

Inside Nyota's mind, a storm raged. Old wounds (Mr. Sims' voice, the secret threats, the shame), mixed with fresh cruelty. That day at school, girls her own age had used casual words like weapons, and those words had found their mark. In her head echoed the lyrics of a Congolese singer: *"If only hearts were little suitcases mothers could open, then she would understand everything I'm carrying inside."* But her heart was locked. Her voice silenced. She lived life like a Zoom call where everyone else could mute and unmute, except her.

"Talk to me, my baby," Bibi pleaded, softening her voice, practicing the gentle language American mothers seemed to use so naturally — a language she herself had never grown up with. "What did they say to you at school?"

Nyota hesitated, then whispered, broken, "One of the girls said I looked like a monkey with these braids. She said I was ugly… because I'm Black."

Bibi's fingers curled into her palm.

Her heart was roaring with the fire of a protective mother, the kind that would march straight into that school and confront every parent, every principal, every child, yet her voice stayed calm and steady.

"You are beautiful, Nyota. You always have been. If anything like that ever happens again, you tell me. I will go to the school. I will talk to whoever I need to."

Nyota's eyes widened in panic. "No, Mama, please don't. Don't go there. Don't say anything."

The thought of her African parents arriving in bold colors, raised voices, and thick accents, embarrassing her, was unbearable. "Just… don't."

Bibi understood that shame. She had tasted it in another form, once. The shame of being called *Nkumba* (barren woman), back in Mbuji-Mayi, before Nyota was born. She knew what it meant to ache for acceptance in a place where humiliation was public currency. But here, they were in America, a country with silent rules she still didn't fully grasp. In Congo, if someone hurt your child, you gathered the entire neighborhood until justice was loud and visible. Here, everything was private, quiet, and restrained. And maybe more violent.

That evening, when Tatu came home and heard what had happened, he simply shook his head.

"Let it go, Nyota. This is nothing. In Africa, bullying was worse, and we survived. These are only words."

Nyota looked down. The words landed like a stone on her shoulders. She knew her father loved her, but his version of love was built on fortitude, not softness. His response did not soothe her. It erased her.

Bibi watched, and something shifted inside her. Tatu wasn't cruel; he had simply never been taught to name emotions. Like so many immigrant parents, he had survived

Melancholy Harmonies

by silence, not by speaking. Their generation had been raised to endure, not to feel.

That night, Bibi slipped into Nyota's room and confessed quietly: "I'm learning too, my child. I didn't grow up with hugs or sweet words. But I want to learn how to stand with you. I may not always get it right, but I see you. I'm here."

Something fragile broke open between them. Nyota still smiled at school, still played basketball, still sang, but her innocence was gone. In its place grew a watchfulness. She became careful, with her hair, her clothes, the parts of herself she showed the world. Her light was now guarded behind glass, burning quietly instead of boldly.

The change grew slowly but became impossible to miss. Nyota began styling her hair to cover her forehead, making sure no strand escaped her careful layers. She laughed less freely, avoided eye contact more often, and weighed every word before opening her mouth. Bibi noticed it all but understood that some wounds have to heal in silence, and that not even a mother can rush the mending.

Then one afternoon, Bibi arrived at school wearing a brightly printed wax dress, full of oranges, emeralds, and sunshine yellows, proud of her culture, unaware she had just walked into a landmine. When Nyota saw her mother among a sea of jeans and neutral sweaters, something inside her snapped.

She wanted to vanish. A wild, burning shame climbed her throat. She wanted to yank her mother away, beg her to change clothes, beg her to stop reminding everyone that Nyota was different. But she said nothing. She swallowed it, head down, hoping no one connected them.

That same day, after school, she got into a fight. It began with a girl staring at her in a way Nyota perceived as mocking. Nyota demanded, "What are you looking for in my face?" The girl didn't back down. Voices rose. Hands almost flew. Other students dragged them apart as Nyota stormed off in the opposite direction, shoulders squared, chin high, rage barely held together.

Beneath all that anger was a thirst, a deep hunger to belong, to be loved, to fit in. When love felt unreachable, she settled for admiration. That, at least, she could earn. She sang angelically, and they applauded. She danced, and they cheered. She excelled, and they praised. She became a master performer, pom-pom squad, choir, academic excellence, anything that secured applause, anything that kept the spotlight bright enough to hide the darkness she carried inside.

But at night, the truth returned. Some nights brought nightmares of shadows, rough hands, suffocating music. Other nights were worse: empty numbness sucking her into silence. When the weight felt unbearable, she thought seriously about ending it, just to stop feeling anything at all.

Her bedroom transformed into a war zone, clothes strewn everywhere, half-eaten plates collecting dust, underwear tangled under homework, candy wrappers beside forgotten worksheets. Bibi begged her to clean, but Nyota ignored her, until one day, Bibi stopped asking and walked into the chaos to do it herself.

That evening, Nyota came home, swung open her bedroom door, and froze.

Her mother was sitting on the edge of her bed, eyes swollen, hands clasped around something small and crumpled in her lap.

"I found this," Bibi said quietly.

Nyota's heart dropped. She didn't need to look. She already knew.

"Yes, Mama," she whispered, her voice flat. "I smoke. That's my weed. It's mine. And I don't want you asking me why."

She lifted her chin, defiant, but her voice trembled beneath the bravery.

Bibi sank further, her fingers fidgeting over the wrinkled rolling papers. She had heard from other African parents that kids in American schools used drugs, but that was their children, fatherless children, or American-born ones. Not her Nyota. Not the miracle girl she had fasted and prayed for through years of barrenness.

Nyota's rage came fast.

"Mama… get out of my room!" she suddenly snapped, eyes wild with a desperate kind of fear. "And please, don't tell Papa. I'm begging you."

Bibi felt her knees turn to water. She rose unsteadily and backed out, not wanting to trigger a further explosion. She knew Tatu's temper, knew if he discovered this now, it could destroy the fragile peace of their home. Better, she reasoned, to absorb it herself, like so many African mothers who become shock absorbers for all the emotion fathers do not know how to hold.

As she closed the door behind her, Nyota slammed it shut. VLAM! Shaking the hallway walls. Bibi clutched her chest, whispering prayers in tongues as she descended the stairs slowly, a new weight pulling at her soul.

Being the child of immigrants is a strange kind of exile. The story that drove Nyota's parents to flee their home country was never spoken of, not around the dinner table, not in casual words. So Nyota pieced together her family history in classrooms, through cold textbook paragraphs about war and genocide. Meanwhile, her teenage emotions battered her from the inside, like a storm she'd never learned how to name.

Nyota retreated deeper into herself.

Some evenings she didn't come straight home after school. She'd wander aimlessly through playgrounds, train stations, basketball courts, anywhere she could be anonymous, anywhere the heaviness inside her could breathe without questions. When she did return, she drifted through the house like a ghost, neither rebel nor obedient child, but something in between: wounded, watchful, unpredictable.

Bibi, terrified of pushing her daughter further away, began choosing her words with surgical care. She no longer scolded about bedtime or homework. Instead, she whispered gentle greetings, left food quietly by the bedroom door, and prayed over Nyota's pillows when no one was watching.

She kept Tatu in the dark, lying by omission, hiding the weed discovery, hiding the sudden drop in grades, hiding even the depth of Nyota's mood swings. She kept telling herself: *When the time is right, I'll tell him. Just not yet. Let me first get our daughter back from whatever darkness is swallowing her.*

Melancholy Harmonies

Tatu, absorbed in work and unfamiliar with the emotional languages of girls, noticed only fragments. When Nyota spoke to him less, he assumed she was becoming a typical American teenager. When basketball trophies stopped appearing, he thought simply: *maybe music has replaced sport.*

But Bibi saw it all: the drifting eyes, the sudden disconnections, the way Nyota's once-vibrant spirit floated just behind her, no longer wearing her skin with pride.

One day, while folding laundry, Bibi whispered into the air: "God, if You saved her from war, from drowning, from abuse… please don't let me lose her now, not when we are finally safe."

She didn't realize Nyota was standing at the top of the stairs, silently watching her mother from behind the railing.

For a flicker of a moment, Nyota's eyes softened. She saw not just a mother, but a woman carrying the weight of survival for them both.

She turned quietly and walked back into her room, closing the door without a slam.

It wasn't healing. But perhaps, just perhaps, it was the first fragile hint of hope.

When Tatu returned that evening, he found Bibi sitting alone at the table, head in her hands, eyes red. He frowned.

"What's wrong? Where's Nyota?"

Bibi looked up, hesitated, then replied slowly, "She's in her room. Things aren't going very well."

Tatu immediately went upstairs. He knocked on the door.

"Nyota? Open up."

No answer. He turned the handle. It was locked. He knocked harder.

"It's me, your father. Open the door."

Long minutes passed. Finally, the door creaked open. Nyota appeared, with a closed face, eyes red from crying or not sleeping. She stepped back. Tatu entered and surveyed the room: the disorder, the smell, the half-open window, the tension.

He wanted to speak calmly, but his words came out like stones.

"What's going on here? Are you smoking now? Do you want to end up like those lost children on the streets of Brooklyn?!"

Nyota crossed her arms. "You don't understand anything. You all don't understand anything."

Tatu felt anger rise within him. He was tired, wounded from surviving the war, from exile, from the humiliation of starting his life over in America, all to give his daughter a better future. And now she was ruining everything?

"I fought to save you, Nyota! Blood, shame, chaos! I lost everything so you could be here! And you... you're smoking?! Why?!"

She looked at him with broken eyes and said the only thing she could say without breaking down: "I hate myself."

The word echoed in the air. Silence fell. Tatu opened his mouth, then closed it. He had no words for this. He loved his daughter, but he didn't understand the invisible pain. Back home in Congo, when something was wrong, people said,

"Be quiet and hold on." But facing this little girl on the brink of young womanhood, he felt... helpless.

"You are my pride," he finally murmured, with a voice like a cracking rock. "Even if you don't believe me."

He awkwardly placed a hand on her shoulder. Nyota didn't back away, but also didn't respond.

That night, Tatu stayed long in the living room, silent. The TV was on, but he didn't watch it. Next to him, Bibi held her Bible, praying softly without stopping. They did not speak, each retreating into their own sense of failure. The house lay still, heavy with silence, like the moment before a storm.

Above their heads, Nyota was lying on her bed, eyes open, still. A thought spun in her mind like a refrain: *If even my parents don't know how to save me... who will?*

The following weeks were a slide. A slow descent rather than a sudden collapse.

Nyota started coming home later and later. She said she had "singing club," "math tutoring," "dance practice," but Bibi knew she was lying. She came back with red eyes, the scent of another world on her clothes — hair, tobacco, sweat, early alcohol.

Tatu closed his eyes. *"It's just a phase... she'll get over it,"* he kept telling himself, but deep down, he was beginning to fear. Fear of losing her for good.

One evening, Nyota forgot her phone on the living room table. Bibi heard a notification ding and, without thinking, grabbed the device. The message blinked on the screen: *"Don't worry, you'll get used to the bottle. You're holding up better than last time, queen."*

Bibi trembled. Bottle? Last time?

Her hands scrolled through the history. What she saw made her blood run cold: videos, stories, photos... Nyota laughing at parties, a beer in her hand, a boy holding her by the waist; Nyota in a bathroom, eyes half-closed, a girl holding a joint between her lips. Bibi felt her knees give way. She sank to the floor, the phone pressed against her chest, crying silently.

When Tatu came home that evening, he found her like that. He took the device, looked at it too, and for the first time in years, he said nothing. He simply stepped outside into the cold, sat on the front porch steps, stared at the street illuminated by streetlights, and cried.

In his tears, he felt something he had not felt since the war: the fear of losing someone in the midst of life.

Nyota, meanwhile, didn't notice the immediate change. She now thought that if she couldn't be loved, at least she could be desired. She dressed shorter, tighter, and more eye-catching. She let boys put their hands on her back, her neck. They told her, "you're sexy," "you're special," two phrases that shut her down more surely than a round of applause.

She danced until exhaustion, drank until she couldn't think anymore. When the pain became too strong again, another girl handed her a small white pill. "Here. You'll float. You'll think less."

She took it. She floated.

She went even lower.

But somewhere beneath this armor of provocation and self-destruction, Nyota hoped for one thing: that someone, an adult, an angel, anyone, would catch her before the final fall.

That an adult, an angel, someone, anyone, would grab her by the shoulders and say: "I love you. Even in your dirt, even in your anger. Come back. You can still come back."

The fall arrived one rainy November evening, without shine or dramatic warning.

Nyota, wearing a red crop-top and ripped jeans, had casually announced that she was going to study at "Amber." But past midnight, she still hadn't come home. Bibi kept glancing at the window. Tatu was pacing around the living room, unable to call the police. How do you tell an American officer that you lost your daughter without seeming to have failed as a parent?

At 1:43 a.m., the phone rang. An unknown number.

"This is St. Mary's Hospital. Your daughter had an incident."

Bibi screamed before she even realized it. Tatu grabbed the keys. The journey felt endless. When they arrived at the emergency room, Nyota was lying down, an IV in her arm, mascara running, wet hair, unconscious. A doctor explained in a neutral voice: "Mild overdose: alcohol, cannabis, pills. She also received a blow to the head from falling in the alley.

She was found in the bushes. If no one had alerted us, she might have…"

He didn't finish. Bibi collapsed. Tatu, stiff, remained standing like a broken tree.

The next morning, when Nyota finally opened her eyes, Bibi sat beside the bed, hands clasped. Tatu held his Bible without reading it.

Nyota saw them. Then she closed her eyes, guilty and ashamed, but too tired to keep up the act.

Her lips moved.

"I'm sorry."

Bibi, her eyes swollen, said nothing. Instead of screams, she simply placed her hand on her daughter's leg.

"We won't let you die, even if you want to die," she murmured.

Tatu stood up. He wanted to speak, but no words came out. He simply placed his hand on Nyota's shoulder and squeezed it, awkwardly, but with all the love he had learned to hide since childhood.

After this episode, everything changed in the Tatu household. Rules were established. Therapy was mandatory, school was monitored, outings were limited. Nyota obeyed the instructions, not out of obedience, but because she no longer had the strength to fight.

The first therapy sessions were exhausting. Nyota remained silent, arms crossed. Then the therapist took out a box of sand and figurines. "If you don't want to talk, build me your world."

Nyota built a desert. A small figure standing alone in the middle. Around it, blurry silhouettes of monsters. And at the very end, a tiny angel with broken wings.

The therapist said nothing. She slowly nodded.

"We'll fix your wings, okay?"

At home, Tatu did something rare: he sat in Nyota's room, saying nothing, just to be there, silently, so she knew she was no longer alone.

Bibi, meanwhile, started cooking dishes from their Congolese childhood: pondu, fufu, and chicken in mwambe sauce. Nyota ate little, but each bite seemed to awaken a forgotten memory.

Music, long abandoned, slowly returned. One evening, Nyota discreetly went downstairs and found her old electronic keyboard. She hesitantly placed a finger on a key... then another... then another.

Bibi, from the kitchen, heard and began to cry. But this time, it wasn't out of pain. It was out of hope.

Life didn't become beautiful overnight.

But something, despite everything, shifted, as if the tide had finally turned.

At high school, Nyota kept her new silence for several months. She floated through the hallways like a fragile presence. She attended classes, did her homework, and spoke to no one. People said she was strange. "She's changed." Yes. She had changed. She had seen the bottom. And now, all her energy went into one thing: survival.

One afternoon, during a group session imposed by the school, students were asked to write anonymously about what they were afraid to show the world. Nyota took her sheet and, with trembling handwriting, wrote: "I'm afraid that my pain is the only thing that defines me."

A few days later, the music teacher, an African-American woman named Mrs. Jenkins, waited for Nyota after class. She handed her a form.

"It's for the 'Youth Voices' contest. I need you to represent the school. Your voice... it carries something others don't."

Nyota wanted to refuse. She was no longer the girl who used to sing. Not after Sims stole that from her.

She replied, "I don't want to do music anymore."

But Mrs. Jenkins didn't give up.

"Then sing your pain. Let it come out. If you keep it inside, it will kill you. Give it to the world. And let God do the rest."

Those words pierced something inside Nyota.

That night, she stayed awake until three in the morning. She wrote. She composed. She cried. Then, at dawn, she had a song. Neither joyful nor sad, but true. Incandescent. Brutal. Beautiful.

She titled her creation: "The Girl Who Survived Herself."

The day of the contest arrived in a theater filled with nervous teenagers, strict teachers, and parents holding up their phones.

When her turn came, Nyota took the stage wearing black jeans and a white shirt. No heavy makeup. No forced smile. Just a guitar and her truth.

She closed her eyes, breathed, and sang.

Her voice was no longer just music; it was a cry transformed into light.

In the audience, Bibi suppressed an emotional sob. Tatu, standing at the back, clenched his teeth to avoid bursting into tears. Even Mrs. Jenkins, usually stern, had her hand on her heart.

At the last note, there was a silence, a silence so dense you could hear tears falling. Then the room erupted in applause. An ovation.

Trembling, Nyota looked around her and smiled for the first time in a very long time.

After the contest, everything unfolded rapidly. Invitations. Doors opening. People wanting to hear her more. Nyota no longer sought the love of others; she wanted to speak her truth. To tell what surviving means.

She made peace with her braids, with her skin, with her name. She began to walk tall again, not because she was healed, but because she had decided that her pain would be her strength, not her prison.

One evening, at the family table, she took her mother's hand. "You know, Mom. I think God let me go through all this so I could sing for those still in the shadows. I realized I am not my shame. I am my testimony."

Bibi burst into tears. Tatu, unable to find words, simply placed his hand on his daughter's, as if to say, "I'm proud," in his way.

Nyota stood up and went to her room, where her notebooks, guitars, and sheet music were now carefully stored. She looked at her reflection in the mirror.

For the first time, she recognized herself.

And for the first time, she chose herself.

Chapter 7

The Day the Silence Spoke

Nyota continued her voice lessons as the years passed, like water flowing steadily under a bridge no one dared cross. She was older now, radiant with a beauty that seemed to sharpen rather than soften with time. But behind her glowing skin and poised posture, she carried a mystery, a hidden weight that threatened to crush her from within. When she sang, she sang with everything in her, pouring out grief and devotion in equal measure. It was not talent that made people cry when she opened her mouth; it was the strange ache of a girl trying to survive her own memories. She poured herself into service to stay busy, to outrun the traumas that crashed into her like waves against a fragile shore.

Every Sunday morning, before the family left for church, Nyota filled the house with melodies so pure they seemed to change the air. On one such morning, Tatu and Bibi stood a few steps behind her, arms folded, simply watching. The service at Hidden Manna Church was surely well underway by now, but she had not noticed. Her fingers moved lightly over the keys as she shifted into *In Christ Alone*, eyes closed, spirit wide open:

In Christ alone my hope is found...
He is my Light, my Strength, my Song...

Melancholy Harmonies

Her fingers never missed a note; her body knew the piano intimately. She didn't even look at the keys. And then, as she began the final verse:

No guilt in life, no fear in death…

Her voice wavered. Tears slipped down her cheeks. Something shifted. She didn't look filled by the Holy Spirit; she looked like a volcano cracking open, years of pain rising from below. Suddenly, Nyota broke. She bent over the piano and began to sob—not soft, polite tears, but a storm of weeping pulled from someplace deep.

"Are you okay, darling?" Bibi asked in alarm.

"Jesus... Jesus..." Nyota whispered hoarsely, trying to gather herself.

"We need to go," Tatu said firmly. "We are very late. We must go and pray with the others."

He rested a hand on her shoulder. Nyota turned, stared into his face, and something erupted inside her. She felt anger rise, irrational, uncontrollable, confusing. She didn't hate her father, but right then, the face of any man felt threatening.

She pushed his hand away and walked to the hallway without a word, past decorative chandeliers still glowing unnecessarily in daylight.

"You can't do this, Nyota," Bibi scolded, following. "Who do you think you are? You will respect your father. In this house, we give you everything."

"That's enough," Tatu interrupted, quietly but with authority. His mind was spinning. Something was very wrong.

"Go... go to church," Nyota wept, wiping at her tears. "Leave me. I'll have my own service here. Just go!"

Tatu took Bibi gently by the arm. "Let's give her space."

They left slowly. Bibi washed her face. Tatu sat in the car with the engine running, staring up at the sky as if hoping God might explain what had just happened.

Alone again, Nyota replayed the moment in her head and covered her mouth in shock. *What have I done?* she thought. She didn't despise her father; what she despised was the image of the male, carved in pain by another man—her abuser. How was she supposed to separate the monster from the innocent? Should she finally tell her parents what really happened to her?

Shaking, she decided to make amends. She wiped her eyes, fixed her hair, and stepped softly into the living room where Tatu now stood near the doorway, still unsure if he should drive off without her.

She approached silently and pressed her head against his back. Bibi, watching from the hallway, held her breath. Nyota wrapped her arms around her father's waist and whispered,

"I'm sorry, Daddy. I'm so, so sorry."

"It's alright, my star," Tatu said, voice thick.

"You forgive me? You really forgive me?" she pressed, her tone almost frantic.

"I already have," he said gently.

"Papa," she added solemnly, "please don't leave me."

"I won't," he promised.

Bibi called from upstairs, "Ken can drive her later, he's always late anyway."

"Oh no, Mama! That's mean," Nyota retorted, almost childlike again.

"Go get ready," Tatu said warmly. "We'll wait."

On the short drive to church, none of them spoke. It was the kind of silence that hums with tension too fragile to name.

"The church has expanded into a much larger parking lot," Tatu mused casually, desperate to talk about anything else.

"Yes," Bibi replied, taking the cue. "They say it cost a fortune."

"The local church is our home," he added. "We must care for it well. It's more than a gathering; it's where God mixes us across tribes and histories."

"You've memorized Pastor Smith's preaching," Bibi said.

***

Tatu flicked off the engine as the church came into view, already swelling with Sunday traffic. Nyota slipped out of the backseat without a word, gliding ahead of her parents just as she used to when she was learning to walk and they trailed behind her like anxious shadows.

She hadn't put her name down to minister that Sunday—no solo, no piano, no choir. Her plan was to remain hidden in the crowd. But anonymity had long deserted her. Nyota was no longer just a member of Hidden Manna Church. She was known. Watched. Expected.

When it was time for the sermon, Pastor Smith Anderson stepped to the pulpit, his smile bright and comforting. He opened the heavy, gold-edged Bible in front of him—he refused tablets and modern screens, always insisting the printed Word must not go extinct. The rustling of the thin pages crackled through the speakers.

He cleared his throat.

"2 Samuel, chapter 13," he thundered, voice suddenly stern. "I read in Jesus' name."

"Amen," responded the congregation.

He began to read the ancient text, the story of Amnon and Tamar. His deep voice rolled over the words like a gavel: *"... Tamar went to her brother Amnon's house... he ordered everyone out... he grabbed her, forced her..."*

Pastor Smith paused dramatically. "Underline that," he instructed. *"He ordered everyone out."*

Nyota's heart stopped.

Those same words stabbed through her mind, dragging up a buried memory: *'Everyone out,'* Mr. Sims had whispered, locking the door before his hands crawled over her small body. She shifted in her seat, throat closing.

Pastor Smith read on. Tamar's pleading. Amnon's violence. The violation. The shame. The command to be silent. Nyota's chest tightened as though she were the one being dragged from that room, dress torn, ash in her hair.

"Do not tell anyone… keep quiet."

Mr. Sims' voice echoed inside her skull, louder than Pastor Smith's. Revenge, rage, horror, everything pounded at once.

Was God speaking to her? Was this some kind of sign? A commandment to finally talk, to shatter her silence? Or was it just her own mind collapsing again?

She could no longer breathe.

Pastor Smith's concluding words rang like an alarm: "When King David heard what had happened, he was enraged, but he did nothing. And Absalom kept silent, hating Amnon from that day." The pastor preached on.

Nyota felt sweat dampen her palms as a single, terrible question rose like fire in her bones: *Would she continue the silence of Tamar... or become the storm of Absalom?*

It felt like two years passed in the scriptures before Pastor Smith resumed reading.

"Absalom held a feast for the sheep-shearers at Baal-hazor. He invited all the king's sons. And when Amnon's heart was merry with wine, Absalom gave his servants this command: 'Strike him down when I give the signal.' And they did."

The sanctuary went silent.

Pastor Smith lifted his gaze slowly, sweeping it across the pews. Every eye was fixed, waiting.

Nyota gripped the edge of her seat. The air felt too thin.

"Only Amnon died that day," Pastor Smith concluded, voice heavy.

A hush rolled through the sanctuary like a curtain being drawn. Then someone at the back whispered, "Praise the Lord."

"Hal-lelujah," murmured the congregation.

Pastor Smith closed his Bible and announced, "The consequences of sin." His eyes flashed momentarily toward Nyota, sharp and piercing.

How does he know? her mind screamed. *I haven't spoken to anyone about Mr. Sim. Can he read my mind? This whole sermon is aimed at me.*

Her breath quickened. Anger and confusion surged. Shame tangled with suspicion. Tears pricked at her eyes, and she wiped them away, pretending it was sweat.

At this point, she could barely hear the pastor.

Pastor Smith's voice finally cut back through her fog: "Amnon's crime led to Absalom's vengeance. Sin produces revenge. But God says, *"Vengeance is Mine... the repayment is Mine."* We must forgive, or the world will never heal."

Around her, people whispered the phrase to each other like a holy echo: *"Sin produces vengeance... Sin produces vengeance..."*

Soon the service dissolved into its usual exodus, one swelling line moving toward the center aisle to greet the pastor and his wife. "Thank you, Pastor." "See you next Sunday." Polite smiles. Warm handshakes. Familiar noise.

Nyota trailed behind her parents in this procession like a shadow shy of the sun. Ahead of them stood Mambu, freshly shaved, his shirt collar starched so stiff it grazed his chin. A tiny dot of blood marked where his razor had slipped. Bibi watched everything with quiet suspicion.

Tatu had often warned her about Mambu, an oily character from Likasi rumored to work with dangerous men back in Congo, always plotting mysterious "projects" with unclear motives.

Now Mambu turned to Tatu with a grin.

"Brother, can I catch a ride home? Came in an Uber," he added casually.

Tatu's face tightened. Bibi nudged him urgently before he said something regrettable. As Mambu quoted the pastor's sermon, *"'Vengeance is the Lord's, we must forgive,'"* he lifted his hands theatrically, smile lingering just a little too long.

Bibi kept watching him.

Men like that, she thought, *come to church only to pretend at righteousness.*

Meanwhile, Tatu remained unusually silent, a silence thick and unfamiliar.

"I suppose that's all I grasped from the sermon," muttered Mambu as they crossed the church courtyard. "The interpreter was going too fast today."

"How could you retain anything," Tatu finally snapped, head shaking in annoyance, "when you spent half the message scrolling on your phone checking Facebook?" He glared. "And since you're looking at me like that, I want to know — you came here with a girlfriend on this trip. Why didn't you bring her to church?"

Mambu dodged the accusation with a slippery change of subject.

"I hear your daughter, Nyota, interprets here too?"

The tactic worked. Tatu's thoughts immediately shifted toward Nyota—the puzzle of her behavior at both church and home remained unsolved and gnawed at him daily.

"Interpreting is no small task," he said, softening. "I'm grateful the church at least has two interpreters, especially since most of the congregation is Afro-American. I suggested the idea myself to Pastor Smith."

"I truly admire that your daughter speaks both languages," Mambu continued. "Most kids I see in diaspora homes only know English."

"Oh, Nyota speaks English, French, and understands Swahili," Bibi added proudly as she bent to retrieve a lost earring, fastening it back to her lobe.

"It took discipline," said Tatu. "At our front door, there's a sign: French starts here, no English allowed beyond the threshold."

"It works," Mambu laughed with approval. "I must tell my cousin to do the same with his children."

Bibi carefully quickened her steps in ten-centimeter heels, placing one foot in front of the other like a dancer balancing over land mines. She overtook the two men, who had paused beneath a tree to argue politics again. As she did, she thought she heard Mambu shout:

"No, no! What peace? What disgusting joke!"

But she had no time—she was hurrying toward Nyota, waiting in the car. All Bibi cared about now was her daughter's well-being and removing these heels stabbing her feet like knives. Home. Food. Rest. Monday morning, work awaited with its daily exhaustion.

She yanked open the backseat door. Nyota sat slanted against the driver's seat cushion, head bowed, left hand clutching the upholstery, right thumb tapping her phone.

"Nyota? You didn't even hear me open the door?" Bibi climbed in, unhooked her stilettos, and rummaged in her purse. Through the tinted glass, she saw the men approaching, hands animated mid-debate.

"No, my dear," Mambu shouted, "not peace! It's a death sentence for the country!"

"You don't even know what you're talking about," Tatu bit back, sliding in behind the wheel and slamming his door.

"Madam, please take the front seat," Mambu politely gestured to Bibi.

"I'll sit behind with my daughter," she answered, settling next to Nyota.

Tatu stared at Nyota in the mirror. "Nyota, what's wrong with you? You won't even greet people now?"

"Hello, Papa," she whispered quickly, eyes still glued to the floor mats as though searching for a lost coin.

Tension settled in the cabin like humidity before a storm. The car smelled of sweat despite cold air blasting from the vents. Tatu's shaved head glistened. Mambu dabbed his own scalp with a handkerchief. Bibi held back a smile; these men could preach peace in church, yet looked ready to strangle each other in the car.

She recalled the last words she had overheard: "No, no, what peace!"

And here they sat, anything but peaceful. Nyota remained motionless beside her, eyes sinking deeper inward. To cut the tension, Mambu tried faux admiration.

"You've got quite a Jeep, my friend."

"Save your flattery," Tatu snapped. "You come spouting nonsense. If Tshisekedi sold the country, why is Kagame angry?"

"It's nothing but political theatre!"

Melancholy Harmonies

"What theatre? Have you known war? Have you collected corpses from the ground? Our children fled death, and now they fight for peace. My daughter behind us works with Action for Congo. She helped push the declaration of Congolese American Day in Washington."

Nyota sat rigid, mysterious, wounded, an arsenal of rage contained within a gifted mind. She excelled at school, led advocacy clubs, fought for her bleeding homeland, and yet something was fractured, private, untold.

"And what's wrong with making deals?" Tatu argued. "After millions are dead, these minerals mean nothing to the ones who've lost!"

"So you sell the country then? said Mambu.

Tatu swerved sharply to the side of an overpass exit, hitting the hazard lights. Cars honked madly as he cried out, "Get out! It's you, you're the ones selling us to hell, traitors!"

Bibi clutched Tatu's arm. "Please, let's just drop him home. Satan wants us to fight. We came straight from church, Tatu!"

Melancholy Harmonies

Nyota stared silently out the window as the world around them spun.

Tatu pulled up finally before a gated apartment building.

"Thank you, brother," Mambu said, fleeing the Jeep, his shirt soaked in sweat.

Bibi scrambled into the passenger seat. Nyota remained in the back, catching the last flicker of Mambu's figure retreating behind the iron gate.

It had been a heavy Sunday, too heavy. Nyota's eruptions, her sudden emotional storms, her secret shutdowns, she carried not only trauma she could not name, but a loneliness fierce as a second skin. Now she nurtured another dream: to start a nonprofit and return home one day to serve child survivors.

"Tread carefully, Congo isn't safe yet," Tatu often cautioned. "Finish your master's degree first."

But Nyota had silently paused that degree. She could no longer bear it, and her parents did not know. She needed space for her sanity, her mental health. *Papa forced me to begin it for his pride,* she told herself. Instead, she'd saved money to launch her foundation.

"You're brilliant," her father always repeated. "Finish school and you'll do anything."

Yet he did not see her turmoil. All her parents offered were survival tools: study hard, get married, be strong.

She worked now, but still lived under their roof, treated as a child.

"You go there to study. Not to play," Tatu would warn before she left for class. She would nod, choking back resentment.

That was the immigrant paradox: raised by Congolese parents on American soil and caught between obedience and personal freedom.

Online, Nyota often saw memes mocking strict African fathers — a Nigerian dad chasing his daughter's boyfriend across a college courtyard, and girls laughing in the comments.

Her father would say lovingly, "One day you will thank us for being strict. Look at these American children, their parents let go too soon. They finish high school, get dumped into fast food jobs, pile up loans, and life begins in debt," Tatu would add with a huff. "All that just to pretend they're independent!" He tapped the steering wheel for emphasis.

"They eat McDonald's for breakfast, lunch, and dinner, guzzle soda like water, and then one day, boom: diabetes, cholesterol, high blood pressure!"

Nyota rolled her eyes discreetly, though inside she simmered.

"At least you won't end up like that. You'll finish school properly, complete your Master's, and have a respectable career."

"Yes, Papa," she whispered, though the life he described felt more like a gilded cage than a destiny.

In her heart, she had already made her decision: pause the degree, take control of her mental healing, and launch her foundation for war-affected children. She wanted to own her future, not be paraded as her father's achievement.

Melancholy Harmonies

"You're staring out the window again?" Tatu asked, catching her reflection in the rearview mirror.

Nyota startled, yanked from her thoughts. "No, Papa... I'm listening," she replied softly, even as her spirit longed to scream.

Another day, Nyota sat stiffly in the living room, half-listening as her father's familiar lecture rolled over her like a tired wave. He was warning again about young people in America who moved out too early, collected traffic tickets, fell behind on rent, and then found themselves bankrupt or evicted by the time they were thirty-five.

"All because they wouldn't listen to their parents," Tatu said, pacing slowly. "They wanted freedom. Flatmates. Fast life. And when everything crashes, when roommates fight and landlords change locks, who do they run back to? Their parents. And yes, we open the door... but with what result?"

Across the room, Bibi moved through the house like a restless spirit, down to the basement tossing clothes into the washing machine, back upstairs to stir a pot on the stove, then into the second-floor sitting room where she gathered stray cups, spoons, fast-food wrappers, and bundles of hair weave. She called down: "Nyota, look at everything I found upstairs in your 'territory!'"

"I know, Mama, okay…" Nyota muttered, exhausted.

"If you want 'freedom' so badly," Bibi said, "you need to be more organized. See how your face is twisting up? I know you're tired of us. But one day you'll understand, we're not the worst parents in the world."

Nyota swallowed hard. *Soon, it will all be over*, she thought. *Soon I won't have to hear these sermons anymore.*

***

Her parents didn't know the truth: that she had quietly stopped her master's program. That university had become unbearable. That every day on campus felt like a quiet death she couldn't describe. But how could she explain that to Tatu? His world revolved around education, not emotions.

One afternoon, she sat frozen on the white leather sofa, staring at her phone as Bibi came flying out of the bedroom, arms raised.

"My God, can't you smell that burning? The pot!"

Smoke billowed from the kitchen. Bibi snatched the scorched saucepan off the stove, tossed it into the sink, and cranked the faucet.

"Where's your father?" she snapped, turning toward her daughter's silent profile.

"Outside," Nyota answered quietly. "Talking to Ken."

"And you didn't smell the smoke? God! You smelled nothing while the house went up in flames?"

Just then, Tatu burst in from the back door.

"What's that smell? Did you burn a pot? Bibi, I left you here in the living room with Nyota!"

Bibi whirled around, her frustration spilling over.

"So now I can't even go to the bedroom if the child is here? You spoil her. You don't teach her how we do things back home in Africa! One day she'll be someone's wife. What kind of woman will she be?"

Irritated, Tatu opened every window to chase out the smoke.

Melancholy Harmonies

"Am I the one who should be watching the pot?" he grumbled. "I stepped outside to handle Ken's dog, always pooping in our yard, and he never cleans it! He must use bags like everyone else and train that animal properly."

Nyota didn't say a word. Earbuds tucked in, phone glowing in her palm, she stared at the floor. She loved tiny white dogs and dreamed of having one in the apartment she hoped to move into someday, a life no one knew she had already planned. But in this moment, with the burned pot and the shouting, all she could feel was shame. In her mind, the house hadn't just filled with smoke; it had nearly burned down, and it was her fault. She wanted to vanish.

"Nyota, what is wrong with you lately?" Tatu demanded. "It's as if you're never really here. When the pot burned, where were you? Listen… you will stay under our roof until someone comes to marry you properly. Don't be like these other African kids who run from home. Even many White families keep their children until they finish college and marry. So stay and behave!"

The words made her heart twist painfully. *Marry… marry… marry*, she repeated silently, pressing her phone to her chest.

The idea filled her with dread, a heaviness she could not explain without falling apart.

Then her mind snapped.

"Oh my God, what have I done?" she wailed suddenly. "Me again, it's always me! The whole house could have burned because of me!"

Her knees buckled. She collapsed onto the leather sofa, sobbing. Tatu rushed to her side, grabbing her hand.

"What did you do to the child?" Bibi shouted, dropping to her knees. "My baby, tell us what's wrong!"

She lay Nyota's head against her chest, pressing her fingers to her pulse as panic rose.

"Call 911, now!" Nyota commanded, her voice breaking.

Nyota clutched her chest, her breathing ragged.

"It hurts, Mama, my chest. Call them! Chest pain!"

Tatu fumbled the phone onto speaker.

"Address, please?" the dispatcher asked.

"3217 North East Street, 73218, hurry!" Tatu barked.

"Why are they asking for the address? Can't they see it on caller ID?" Bibi cried.

"This is not the time for questions!" Tatu snapped.

Outside, sirens wailed.

"They're here! They're here!"

Paramedics rushed in with a stretcher.

"Chest pain? How old?"

"Twenty-four."

"Family history?"

Nyota was placed on the stretcher, an oxygen mask pressed to her face, electrodes attached to her chest.

"Heart rate 144. Tachycardic. She's short of breath."

"Overdose?" someone asked.

"No," Tatu snapped. "She studies well. She's a good girl. Why is her heart racing?"

Melancholy Harmonies

***

Bibi stood trembling in the hospital hallway, hands pressed to her temples. Déjà vu washed over her violently, not visual, but aural. Years ago, back in Congo, Nyota had wailed inconsolably in the night as a baby. The village pediatrician had examined her and said the same words now ringing through the ER: "Everything looks normal."

She turned to Tatu, whispering through tight lips, "They told us that back then... and they tell us the same today."

Tatu stared at the floor.

"And what about blood?" he asked the nurse.

Nyota, overhearing, suddenly snapped, "Papa, I'm fine! Please, just go home!"

There was a wildness in her voice. She didn't want them there, not out of cruelty, but because something was pushing its way up from the darkest part of her chest, demanding to be spoken, now or never. *If I don't let it out, I'll die*, she thought. *At least here, in this hospital, maybe someone would understand, not judge.*

The nurse intervened gently.

"Could you please wait outside? The room is too small, we'll update you."

Nyota exhaled sharply as her parents were ushered out. Tears flooded her eyes. At last, the door closed, and a nurse drew the curtain.

"Are you okay? Do you need anything?" the nurse asked.

Nyota shook her head fiercely.

"Please," she whispered, voice breaking, "don't let my parents come back in. Please, send them away."

"Your father has gone home. Your mother is just in the waiting area," the nurse assured her.

Nyota clutched the edges of the hospital blanket. Her chest still ached, not from illness, but from the weight of a truth she had swallowed for too long. The fluorescent lights above hummed. On the monitor, her vitals slowly steadied, her breathing quieted. But inside, something had cracked open. She felt herself on the edge, between survival and surrender.

Her fingers tangled in her hair.

It's time, she thought.

***

Nyota's eyes were swollen from crying as she got up and crept toward the glass door, peering anxiously down both sides of the corridor, as if to verify what the nurse had just told her. Seeing neither of her parents, she returned slowly to the bed. The nurse stepped closer.

"You are safe here. I'm listening," she said gently.

Nyota sniffled. "Earlier, when you asked if I'd been abused or used marijuana, and I said no." Her voice trembled, "I lied. My parents don't know. I was abused when I was a child."

"Thank you for opening up," the nurse replied softly.

Nyota nodded, staring down at her fingers. "Please, don't tell my parents. They can't know."

There was a soft knock on the glass door. Nyota nearly jumped. "Oh no, is that my mom?"

"No, it's not her." The nurse placed a reassuring hand on her arm. "You're an adult. We respect your privacy. The doctor who assessed you called in a psychologist. She's here just for you."

A Black woman entered, slim and poised, wearing a green dress just above the knee, tucked beneath a white coat left casually unbuttoned. Her skin was smooth, her smile dazzling, and her natural hair pulled back into a neat puff. She set her laptop down and pushed her glasses up her nose.

"Hi Nyota," she said warmly, pronouncing the name perfectly. "I'm Dr. Tameka Jackson, but you can call me Dr. Tameka."

Melancholy Harmonies

Nyota blinked. *She looks like me,* she thought. *If I took off this wig and wore my real hair... I could look just like her.*

"Tell me," Dr. Tameka said, pulling up a chair. "What brought you here today, Nyota?"

Something about hearing her name spoken correctly unlocked Nyota's chest. She felt the walls themselves leaning in to listen. For a moment, she resisted, then everything inside her swelled. Two worlds waged war inside her—one where she had a divine mission, a destiny, and another whispering death, shame, uselessness. *Sometimes I think no one really loves me,* she confessed silently. *What's the point in living?*

"Have you ever had suicidal thoughts?" the doctor asked gently.

Nyota hesitated, then answered with surprising clarity. "Sometimes thoughts crash into each other in my mind... but I've never had the courage to end my life. I believe I'm meant to do something greater in this world, even through this pain, the sleepless nights, this... chaos."

Dr. Tameka nodded slowly, recognizing the strength shining through the brokenness. She listened without interrupting as

Nyota spoke, crying, breathing, glancing up at the ceiling, then back to her knees, dabbing tears.

Finally, Nyota stopped, emotionally spent. The doctor handed her a cup of water.

"Would you like me to refer you to ongoing therapy?" she asked. "I know someone excellent, Mrs. Tamisha Owens. And we have psychiatrists… people with experience, not just training. You won't have to carry this alone anymore."

"Will she be like you?" Nyota asked meekly.

The doctor smiled. "Maybe even better."

Nyota exhaled a long breath. "Thank you."

She was given discharge papers and a referral for therapy. A part of her didn't want to leave. This room felt like the first safe place she had known in years, but the nurse gently walked her back toward the waiting area, where Bibi had been sitting with a haunted, anxious face.

When Bibi saw her, she stood up immediately and pulled her daughter into her arms.

"Are you okay? What did they say? What about your tests?"

Nyota leaned into her mother but kept her voice controlled. "I'm fine. They said it's stress. I just... I need rest. I think I need to travel. Alone. Somewhere."

Bibi felt her heart tighten. Her daughter was slipping away, not physically, but spiritually, emotionally drifting to somewhere she couldn't follow. Independence was expected at her age, but Bibi's deepest fear was that Nyota was suffering in silence, and she had no idea how to reach her anymore.

***

Summer in Dallas was unforgiving. The heat pressed down like the lid of a furnace, hot enough to melt rubber, hot enough to steal breath. Every evening, the local news delivered fresh tragedy — children fainting on playgrounds, elderly folk collapsing at grocery store entrances. One mother, staggering into her shift at a clinic, had forgotten her infant in the backseat. By the time she remembered, the baby had already suffocated in the boiling car.

Nyota's mother, Bibi, watched these reports in silence. She had lived through war, seen death crawl across villages dressed in machetes and gunfire — but this, somehow, felt just as cruel. *People dying simply because the sun was too close?* How could anyone make peace with that?

It was said that summers in Texas could last ninety days without a drop of rain. But this year was different. Blistering heat would stretch for weeks, then a sudden downpour would arrive without warning — flooding streets, tearing up highways, drowning entire neighborhoods. Some church folk whispered it was prophetic, a sign of the end times, God shaking the skies to remind humanity that no one truly knew the day or the hour.

Then came a story Bibi could not shake. Over a hundred children were swept away when a religious retreat was hit by a freak flash flood. One of the boys came from the special-needs center where she worked. The news left her hollow. "How can a child die while seeking God?" she whispered to herself over and over, as if the question itself were a kind of rosary.

She drove home from work in a daze. The center worked with "children with special needs," though Bibi often thought the phrase a lie. Wasn't everyone living with some kind of need? Some visible, others buried so deep that only God could see them trembling? These American

Melancholy Harmonies

expressions, special needs, mental health, trauma-informed, swirled in her head. She had survived Congo's wars with no such language, and yet she bore inside her all the symptoms.

Her old Toyota, bought in cash to avoid the trap of American credit systems, rattled as she turned into their tree-lined street. Just ahead, traffic slowed to a crawl. She frowned until she noticed everyone had stopped to let a tiny creature cross. A turtle, she realized, inching across the blistered road in slow motion. Bibi smiled sadly. *In Kinshasa, someone would have kicked it or cooked it.* But here, cars waited patiently. She eased forward and reached her garage.

That evening, she and Tatu ate together in silence. Despite decades in America, Tatu refused to abandon fufu. "African food keeps us healthy. I refuse to balloon like Kabunji!" he'd say.

Bibi teased him in return, "Your semolina isn't as organic as you think."

Minutes passed, bowls scraped empty. Tatu finally spoke.

"Where has Nyota disappeared to this summer?"

Bibi didn't look up from rinsing dishes. "She braids hair at that salon for a few hours, then says she's studying at the library."

"So why doesn't she pick up my calls?"

"Send her a text. You know she always answers faster that way."

"I hate texting. These children want to re-educate us."

Bibi dried her hands, walked to the kitchen counter, and gasped. "Oh my God!"

Tatu jolted. "What?"

"This number called me ten times today!"

"It's scammers. Delete it," he muttered.

"No... something feels important." She scrolled to the voicemail. *"Dear Bibi, it's Ana, your Indian friend... I'm so happy I found your number."*

She pressed play and froze. A thin scream broke from her lips.

Tatu leapt up. "What happened? Who was that?"

Bibi sat, trembling. "No… God, no… not this."

"Tell me!"

"It's Nyota," she whispered. "No… I mean… it's not her. It's… the music teacher…"

Tatu's face drained. "What about Nyota?!"

"She's okay. I think she's on her way home. It's not her… it's not my baby… but they've arrested the music teacher. He was abusing children. They've begun calling parents who used to send their kids there. They want statements… testimonies…"

Her voice cracked. She staggered to the bathroom, leaving her phone on the couch. Tatu grabbed it and dialed back the number without hesitation.

On the other end, a woman answered softly, "Hello?"

"This isn't Bibi. I'm her husband."

There was a brief silence on the line.

Oh… hello, sir," the woman said politely. "I'm Ana. I used to take my daughter for piano lessons years ago with the same teacher as your Nyota. I've just heard he's been arrested. They're reopening everything. The police have my statement, and they may contact you too, just so you aren't taken by surprise."

Tatu's jaw flexed. "Thank you," he said quietly, though his heart thundered. He hung up as Bibi returned from the bathroom, eyes red, cheeks damp.

"Who was that woman?" he asked.

Bibi hesitated. "Just someone from before. You remember… the Indian lady, her daughter Ashley…"

"They called you before calling me," Tatu said, his voice calm but lined with suspicion.

Bibi's gaze fell to the floor. "Because they know the mothers. We were the ones who took our children and waited during those lessons…"

Tatu's nostrils flared.

"Why didn't you tell me sooner?"

"I only found out now!"

"Are you sure Nyota is okay? Is there something she has not told us?"

The question hung between them like a sword. Bibi's stomach twisted. She thought back to Nyota's mysterious mood swings. The anxiety. The sudden crashes. The insistence on privacy. *Had this happened to her… and she kept it from us?*

Tatu grabbed his car keys. "I'm going to pick her up."

"No!" Bibi stepped forward, blocking the door. "Don't go now, you might scare her. She should tell us on her own terms."

"I have the right to protect my child!"

"Protect her by listening first," Bibi pleaded. "The police will contact us if they need to. Don't go barging in and make her hide even deeper."

Tatu's shoulders sagged under the weight of uncertainty. He looked away, gritting his teeth.

That night, they slept restlessly. Bibi kept waking, staring down the hallway toward Nyota's closed bedroom door. Tatu lay on his side, eyes open in the dark, a thousand what-ifs chasing each other across his mind. But Nyota never came out.

In the morning, she was already gone.

When Bibi returned from the bathroom, her heart nearly stopped at the thought that Tatu might have seen the message on her phone. She scanned his face for any hint — suspicion, anger, confusion, but he looked completely indifferent as he finished his meal. She forced herself to breathe.

The mothers of the newly identified victims had planned a brunch the next morning at a quiet downtown restaurant — 10 a.m., just the three of them: Ana, Lisa, and Bibi. They had known one another for years, back when their children attended piano classes. Tatu wanted no part of it. Even the mention of the scandal made him grimace. Nyota, for her part, refused to let them say a word in her presence.

That night stretched into eternity. Bibi tossed and turned, nausea climbing her throat. She kept checking her phone obsessively: rereading texts, playing soft worship music, praying for sleep that never came. Her heart pounded so fast she thought it might explode.

In the morning, she told Tatu she was "going to visit Ana" and wouldn't make it to work. He looked at her as though she'd gone mad, but he offered no protest. He sensed something was being hidden from him... but chose silence.

Bibi was the first to arrive. The restaurant had a calm, thoughtful atmosphere, with round tables spaced widely apart, faux-vintage paintings, and quiet music overhead. On one wall was a mural of a stern-looking bearded man's face. It stirred something in her, a memory buried beneath years of survival. An image from the Kivu. A murderer Nyota had once described in a fever dream. She blinked hard, forcing herself to stay present.

"Would you like some coffee?" the waitress asked softly, startling her.

"Yes... yes, please," Bibi answered in French-accented English, while texting the women to let them know she had arrived.

Coffee had become her lifeline in recent weeks, a jolt to help her battle back terror.

Melancholy Harmonies

She checked the time, 8:46 a.m. The invitation had said ten o'clock. She had completely lost track of reality.

At 9:50, the door chimed, and two women hurried inside. Ana went first, the Indian mother, her once-gleaming skin now dull, dark circles carved beneath her eyes, a long silver-grey silk dress hanging awkwardly on her exhausted frame. Beside her, Lisa, hair cropped and blonde, wrinkles carved into her forehead deeper than Bibi remembered. They looked devastated.

The three women met in a wordless embrace: shoulders shaking, noses sniffing, hands rubbing backs. A sympathetic waiter placed a box of tissues on the table. When they finally sat, Bibi's untouched coffee was already cold. She asked for a glass of water without ice. They brought it full of ice anyway, as Americans always did.

"This is… incredible," Lisa whispered, barely audible. Ana and Bibi exchanged a shattered glance.

"It's terrible," Ana murmured. "Our daughters were abused right under our noses, and they carried that for years… in silence."

She sounded like a woman making a confession.

"This is a serious child protection case," Lisa said quietly.

Bibi stiffened. Her mind reeled. Police? Investigations?

Lisa began recounting, step by step, how the truth had finally surfaced after nineteen years. Her nephew Stephen, who had been five at the time, had eventually told his mother: Mister Sims had touched his genitals during piano class. The mother immediately called the police, and within days, more and more now-adult students began stepping forward with the same story. They were coming from everywhere, saying they too had been abused, but had never dared to tell anyone.

"He'd touch them, and they'd touch him back, and he told them: 'keep quiet or be ashamed forever'," Lisa whispered, eyes brimming. "He stole their childhoods... and now their lives are chaos, drugs, uncontrolled sex, rage, identity confusion..."

It was like a funeral. Every sound in the café turned distant. These were not just other people's daughters; these were their daughters. Nyota.

Everything Lisa described sounded exactly like what Nyota was going through. Except Bibi had never, not once, spoken of sexuality with her daughter. She had missed every sign. Her head throbbed.

The more they thought about it, the worse their heads hurt. A total feeling of denial in the face of a horrible reality right in front of them. Were they really sitting in the downstairs living room while their little girls were being abused upstairs by the staircase? Would they simply vanish into thin air while the monsters devoured their children?

Bibi took a Tylenol from her bag. The other two asked for some as well. They swallowed the pills like a host, like a communion wafer.

Outside, the sky turned gray, with clouds foretelling rain and thunderstorms.

"It's not even the rainy season!" said Bibi, looking outside with her hands on her temples. "It's not even supposed to rain today! This is the end of the world!"

She was talking to herself. She didn't know what to say. In fact, she felt like falling to the ground and crying out loud, the way they did in Africa: "bana ni haribishiya mutoto wangu," meaning, *They have destroyed my daughter.*

"How will I tell my husband?" Bibi whispered at last, terrified. Her fingers fluttered compulsively as she applied lip balm to her dry mouth.

"I don't know either," Ana sighed. "My Anila has mood swings, isolation…" Her voice broke.

"This is witchcraft," Bibi burst out, her voice rising. "This man bewitched our babies. Oh my God, how will I tell Tatu?" She clutched her fingers together, muttering in Swahili, "bana ni haribishiya mutoto!" (Meaning, "they have ruined my child.")

"You must prepare your husbands," Lisa said firmly. "Because you will receive a summons. A blue-stamped letter from the Texas Department of Criminal Justice. Bibi, you work with children. You know how serious child abuse is here. This is just the beginning."

Ana gasped. Lisa reached into her bag and pulled up a local news clip on her phone: Mr. Sims, handcuffed and escorted by police.

Bibi felt faint.

"I have to see Nyota before I go home," she said, standing abruptly.

She found Nyota later that afternoon in the library parking lot.

Nyota looked instantly alert.

"Mom, did you see the news? Everyone is talking about it."

"Yes," Bibi croaked. "Your father still doesn't know…"

"He will," Nyota said, steady. "But don't worry. I've already booked therapy sessions. I am fighting my demons, Mama. You taught me that when I was only a baby. I will not be destroyed."

Tears streamed down Bibi's cheeks.

"Come with me to therapy next time," Nyota added softly. "You need healing too. Dad does too. These demons of abuse chase all of us, but they will not win!"

"I'll find the courage to tell your father," whispered Bibi.

Melancholy Harmonies

Nyota slipped back into the library. Bibi sat alone in her Toyota, engine idling, watching her daughter disappear behind the glass doors, heart breaking anew.

That night, Bibi did not speak. The next morning at 11 a.m., she walked barefoot, trembling, bonnet still on her head, to the mailbox. Her fingertips were icy as she pulled out a single envelope bearing a blue government stamp: TEXAS DEPARTMENT OF CRIMINAL JUSTICE.

Her knees almost gave way.

Hands shaking, Bibi carried the envelope inside as though it were a ticking bomb. Tatu was in the living room, watching a political talk show on YouTube, the volume turned up. She slipped past him quietly and locked herself in the downstairs bathroom, the letter pressed against her chest. Her breathing was uneven as she peeled it open slowly, painfully.

Inside was a formal notice:

"You are hereby requested to make yourself available for questioning as part of an ongoing investigation into child sexual abuse carried out by Mr. Harold Sims (DOB: xx/xx/xxxx). Parents or guardians of any minors who

attended piano or voice lessons under the said individual between 2004 and 2008 are required to comply..."

Bibi covered her mouth in horror. They knew. The government knew. There was no running from it now. Suddenly, her stomach lurched, and she bent over the sink, barely managing not to vomit.

She stayed in the bathroom a long time, too long, until she heard Tatu's voice calling, "Bibi! Everything okay in there?"

She splashed water on her face, composed herself, then stepped out slowly with the envelope tucked inside her prayer shawl. "I'm fine," she answered weakly.

Her cell phone buzzed. A message from Ana: *"Did you receive the blue letter?"* Bibi didn't dare text back.

All day, she played her role mechanically — cooking, cleaning, putting on her headwrap. But her mind was drowning.

How do I tell him? How do I say we failed our child? Will he blame me? Will he blame Nyota?

Melancholy Harmonies

That evening, Nyota appeared for dinner. Hair in a tight bun, face carefully expressionless. Tatu tried to joke with her about politics as they ate fufu and okra stew, but Nyota barely responded. Bibi watched them both, her heart aching.

After the meal, Nyota stood to leave.

"Nyota," Bibi said softly. "Stay. I... I need to talk to you and Papa."

Nyota turned slowly, as if she already knew exactly what was coming.

Tatu looked confused. "What's going on?"

Bibi's voice trembled. "I received a letter today... from the Department of Criminal Justice."

Tatu frowned. "Department of what?"

She pulled the envelope from under the cushion and handed it to him with both hands, like an offering. He snatched it, opened it, and went absolutely still. His eyes scanned the words. Twice. Three times. His jaw tightened, his face paling by the second.

"What... is... this?!" he thundered.

Nyota flinched. Bibi burst into tears.

"Tatu, please, listen. It's about Mr. Sims, the music teacher. They've arrested him…"

"Why is our name on the letter? What does this have to do with us?" he yelled.

Nyota stood frozen near the door, her skin crawling.

"Tatu… our daughter… she…" Bibi couldn't finish.

Tatu's eyes shot toward Nyota, suspicion, disbelief, and fear mixing together at once. Nyota's breathing quickened. She opened her mouth, but no sound came out.

"What are you telling me? That my child…" His voice cracked. He turned away, clutching his head. "Bibi, why didn't you tell me sooner? Where was I? Where was I?!"

He began pacing like a lion trapped in a cage.

"I didn't know…" Bibi sobbed. "She didn't tell us. She was a child…"

Nyota stepped forward, tears finally spilling silently down her cheeks.

"Papa..." Her voice was barely above a whisper. "It happened... when I was six. I was afraid. He told me you would be ashamed. That you would never love me again. So I kept quiet."

Tatu froze mid-step. His entire body began to shake. He pressed both hands to his face, then let out a roar so raw Bibi thought the neighbors might hear it. He staggered backward until he hit the wall and collapsed slowly to the floor, head in his hands.

"My daughter... my only daughter... oh God..." he wept.

Nyota knelt awkwardly beside him, not too close, those old fears still lingering. But she extended her fingers and lightly touched his shoulder.

"I... I'm sorry, Papa. I wanted to protect you."

Tatu looked up at her with swollen red eyes, grief and guilt destroying him.

"You were a child... I was supposed to protect you," he cried. "And I failed."

The three of them sat in that living room, bathed in anguish and silence. Years of buried pain rose like smoke from a hidden fire. No one spoke. No one had words.

Finally, Bibi whispered, "We will go together. To the police. To testify. We won't be silent anymore."

Tatu nodded slowly, a broken man, but a father ready to stand up again.

Nyota looked from one parent to the other, and for the first time in years, she allowed herself to believe that maybe healing was possible.

It was a week disrupted by headaches and insomnia. They were expected to go to a center where police officers worked alongside psychologists and forensic nurses. Tatu could not hide the trembling in his hands. His legs kept moving on their own. He had never imagined himself there, speaking about his daughter's body to strangers. Shame mixed with rage in his chest.

The investigators questioned each victim separately, while the parents, left waiting endlessly, could barely endure it.

"Oh my God! They might come to arrest us too. Why are they taking so long? What's happening?" Bibi whispered.

Ana, Anila's mother, sat beside her and leaned in close. "I heard our children will have to undergo thorough medical examinations afterward," she murmured.

That was too much. Bibi's vision blurred, her body giving way as she nearly collapsed from her chair. Tatu caught her just in time, gripping her as she sagged toward the floor. She wanted to vanish from the room. Her breathing came fast and shallow.

"Hold on," Tatu murmured, even as something inside him collapsed too.

The parents' interrogation went less dramatically than they had feared. They were asked simply to explain the facts as they were. Yes, they had been waiting for their children at the bottom of the stairs, while upstairs, behind the sounds of music, stories they would never have suspected were unfolding.

What embarrassment!

They were all there, faces defeated, waiting for the verdict on the monstrous culprit and their entry into therapy and counseling sessions.

In the days that followed, they all had to appear before a judge at the Department of Justice in the federal building downtown. Tatu and Bibi felt as if they had stepped into one of the courtroom scenes they had seen on TV in the show *Mr. Judge*. Bibi pinched herself; she still couldn't quite believe this nightmare.

The judge, stern-faced, recited the charges one after another, raised his gavel, and struck it hard.

The arrest was immediate. Mr. Sims was handcuffed that very day. In court, dressed in orange, he walked with his back bent, hands behind him, eyes down. He did not deny anything.

There was nothing to deny. He had pleaded guilty under the fixed gazes of parents lined up behind their traumatized children. Nyota buried her face in Bibi's knees. She hurt for her parents, because she knew that for them, this was the beginning of a trauma she had endured alone for a very long time.

Sims was sentenced to thirty years in prison at the age of sixty-four. Upon hearing the verdict, Tatu, seemingly unmoved, broke down once he got home. He rushed into the bathroom, closed the door, and sobbed like a child, hitting the wall until his knuckles bled.

"How could I let this happen? How did I not see it?" he kept repeating.

The rebuilding was slow and painful.

Chapter 8

When Healing Took Her Hand

Mrs. Tamisha Owens was unlike any therapist Bibi had imagined. Gentle, elegant, and deeply spiritual, she was a Christian counselor married to a white pastor and had served for over twenty years in a town two hours outside Dallas. Bibi knew she could not involve her husband in this stage of the journey, not now when he was already overwhelmed by events, especially the police summons. Tatu dismissed anything to do with abuse as sensationalist, exaggerated, or downright false. He was in total denial. In his mind, going to therapy meant being a loser. He needed time to come around.

"Never my daughter!" he thundered each time the subject arose. "Leave her alone. She's doing well at school. Mood swings? We all have them. I don't want to hear any more of this!"

Bibi often thought, without daring to say it aloud, *"Your uncontrollable anger is proof you need therapy too."* But she kept her famous silence, a silence that could smother wildfires like water thrown over embers. She did not want to oppose her husband and spark needless battles. For now, her only priority was to sit quietly in front of the therapist with Nyota at her side. Every second mattered. In America, sexual abuse of minors was not just a scandal; it was a federal matter that could cling to a family for life. Her legs trembled just thinking about the consequences of that dreadful letter. Nyota sat beside her, mute throughout the drive. Bibi wondered what thoughts churned inside her. Maybe she was preparing to speak, finally, she hoped. *Please God, let her speak today.*

Inside the warmly lit therapy office, Mrs. Owens sat across from Nyota with a compassionate patience that seemed carved out of heaven itself. This was only their second session. The first had ended abruptly, Nyota too afraid to open the locked vault of her memories.

"What do you think people believe about you?" Mrs. Owens asked, her voice soft and angelic.

Nyota clenched her jaw before the dam broke. "I hate myself for being a Black girl," she blurted. "And worse, I feel filthy. At school, some people tell me Blackness wasn't made for anything good." Her shoulders shook as sobs consumed her.

Mrs. Owens inhaled slowly. "I know how painful it is to talk about childhood memories that carry shame."

Melancholy Harmonies

Nyota gave a bitter smile. "Exactly. When that girl mocked me at school, all my bad memories rushed back. Disgust filled me. I learned to fake my image, to be confident, stylish, brilliant at sports and at school, so no one would guess how broken I really am. I've always wanted to know where I come from. The day a teacher lectured on rape as a weapon of war, I searched on Google for Congo, the country where I was born. My parents never told me…" Her voice trailed off. "I read about babies and children killed or raped in front of parents too helpless to protect them. I wrote it all down in my journal."

Mrs. Owens leaned forward. "How do you feel knowing your parents escaped that tragedy and brought you to America?"

Nyota's eyes widened, as if a door had snapped open. "I… I don't know how they managed it. My mother once told me a tiny bit about how invaders stormed our house one night. It sounded like some fairy tale. But I've dreamt for years of people trying to kill me. And what happened here with my music teacher, it messed me up even more. I Googled it, post-traumatic stress disorder. Big words, huh? All I know is I shut down. I wanted the ground to swallow me whole."

Nyota paused to wipe her face. Her fingers trembled. "Someone at school gave me marijuana once. Said it would help me sleep… help my mind. But the more I smoked, the more anxious, jumpy, paranoid I became. I stopped cleaning my room. I stopped doing anything. I was exhausted all the time. My life turned into a mess, inside and outside." She let out a nervous little laugh. "Sorry… I've said too much again today. My mom's probably in your chapel praying for me right now."

Silence settled, dense and holy. Mrs. Owens let it breathe before she replied, quoting softly:

"Isaiah 41:10: 'Do not fear, for I am with you; do not be dismayed, for I am your God. I will strengthen you and help you; I will uphold you with My righteous right hand.'"

They had already spent far longer in therapy than scheduled, but Mrs. Owens never looked at her watch. Time bowed itself to healing.

"I'm sorry," Nyota whispered. "I know you must have other appointments."

Mrs. Owens shook her head. "This moment is for you. You've carried your burden alone for too long. From now on, that stops."

Bibi met Nyota in the waiting room and wrapped her arms tightly around her. To her astonishment, Nyota did not pull away this time. For the first time in years, she melted into her mother's embrace. Bibi wept silently behind Nyota's back, understanding that something sacred had just taken root.

At the next session, Mrs. Owens gave Nyota an assignment: to write a letter, not to herself, not to her parents, but directly to the music teacher who had abused her. "Another girl, Ashley," she explained, "also wrote a letter to her abuser during therapy. It released something powerful inside her."

Nyota agreed. That night, she poured her heart out on paper:

Melancholy Harmonies

Criminal,

Today, I choose to shed the past you forced upon me when I was just a child, wanting only to play with my toys. You twisted my mind, made me believe I existed to serve your perverted desires. You brainwashed me with gifts, candies, and lies about my parents not loving me like you did. You, a 59-year-old man, dared to put your filthy hands and thoughts on children aged 4 to 6.

You are the devil himself; no other name fits. I speak not just for me, but for all the little ones whose lives you poisoned.

You made some of my friends believe sex was all they were worth. You caused emotional, spiritual, and physical torment that can barely be written. Because of you, I wet my bed at twelve. I vomited at night. I used drugs just to forget. You stole our innocence and damaged our destinies.

But I am rising in the power of Christ. I pretend to be happy, but inside I have been shattered, like Ashley and Anna and all the daughters whose dreams you strangled. Where was God when you cast your spell on us? Why were we your prey? I pray that the voices of survivors will grow louder every day until justice falls like thunder.

This letter is only the beginning. Let every victim of childhood abuse know this: you are not dirty. You were chosen to shine, and that is why evil targeted you early. Now rise and speak. You are not alone."

Mrs. Owens blinked back tears while reading the letter. Nyota had chosen not to remain a victim but a warrior. Guided by Scripture, therapy, and raw honesty, she began to reclaim herself. Genesis had once shaken her when she thought humans evolved from apes, echoing cruel taunts from school. Now she understood differently. God had created her, intentionally, beautifully, not as an accident, but as a miracle.

The letter became a turning point. For years, Nyota had swallowed words that had poisoned her from the inside. Now, putting them on paper released the venom. She read the letter aloud in Mrs. Owens' office, her voice breaking, but she finished every line. When she was done, the silence was thick and holy again, but this time it carried strength rather than despair.

Mrs. Owens leaned forward. "Do you see what you've done? You've broken his hold. You've named his evil and refused to carry it as your shame any longer."

Nyota's shoulders sagged, as if a heavy cloak had been removed. She stared at her trembling hands and whispered, "For the first time, I feel... clean."

The therapy sessions continued. Gradually, Nyota was enlightened through Bible study, therapy, stories, and emotional expression. She rejected false narratives that linked evil to certain races. The man who had assaulted her was Caucasian, married to a Korean woman. Children of Black, Indian, and Asian descent had all been victims. Many other children are, and still are, silenced by abusers who make them believe, "No one will believe you." Some abusers go as far as mentally dominating their victims until the child trusts the abuser more than their own parents.

Nyota shared Genesis 6:6 with Mrs. Owens: *"The Lord regretted that he had made human beings on the earth, and his heart was deeply troubled."*

She finally understood that God did not create the world with the intention of controlling it. On the contrary, He created man and woman with the freedom to submit to His will or not.

"He doesn't force anyone for salvation," Mrs. Owens clarified. "It's the devil who oppresses and manipulates minds. Sin took root in the Garden of Eden, where God had given everything to man and woman to enjoy, yet they were tempted by the forbidden fruit tree. Every nation and race has its own struggles and demons to fight since sin entered the world. Since we all share the same blood, we all carry the same sinful tendencies. If we cannot avoid succumbing to temptation, the good news is that, through Jesus' blood, we have obtained forgiveness for our past and future sins."

Nyota had long struggled with issues of identity because of false ideas her friends spread about Black people. These friends had invited her to join movements that claimed she had her own gods and ancestors. Nyota was beginning to question her ancestry and the meaning of "new birth" in Christianity.

"We all are born with a dark side," said the therapist. "And when we come to Christ, we change our behaviors for the better. That's why it's called 'the new birth.' We desperately need this new identity in Jesus because we all tend to act or think badly. This tendency is the sin we find hard to control. Did you know that two-year-old children naturally lie to avoid punishment? Who taught this little child to lie? It is natural, original. To be saved, we need to follow Jesus to ensure a good eternal life after this earthly one."

"Each race has its own traditions and inherited flaws from ancestors," Mrs. Owens continued. "We should not only reject the bad things from our ancestors but also renew our minds and our being, and be baptized in water and Spirit. We must keep traditions aligned with God's will and reject those that are synonymous with abuse, lies, violence, and other wrong actions. No race is superior to another in God's eyes. In fact, all races have sinned and are deprived of God's glory.

Do not deny your ancestral roots, for they are part of your identity. Generational curses do not only affect Black people. Victims of the Holocaust also carry much ancestral trauma. For true freedom, each individual is called to receive Jesus Christ as Lord and Savior."

Nyota listened attentively and silently to everything Mrs. Owens said. Now, she had much to digest and meditate on from this encounter.

"How do you find this so far?" asked the therapist.

"It's fantastic and, at the same time, overwhelming to hear another version of the story!" she replied. "I want to go further and process all this. Do my parents know this story of redemption through Jesus Christ? I wish someone had told me before. I'd love to come back and hear more."

"That was only a small excerpt, a preview of the immeasurable work of salvation accomplished on the cross by Jesus Christ. Next time, we'll have more stories to tell," concluded the therapist.

Nyota agreed to accept Jesus Christ and asked to be baptized willingly. She was curious about the Holy Spirit. Someone had told her that water baptism would unlock her spiritual gifts and talents. She had memorable encounters with the Holy Spirit in her dreams and often experienced prophetic and premonitory visions while asleep. Yet she confided in her mother that she had been secretly trying to understand her future by drawing tarot cards.

The hymns at church pierced her differently now. Words she had once dismissed as empty suddenly shimmered with meaning. When the choir sang, *"Amazing grace, how sweet the sound, that saved a wretch like me,"* Nyota wept openly. She was no longer weeping out of confusion or fear, but because she understood: grace was not just for others. It was for her.

At home, she resumed greeting her mother and sharing meals. Bibi didn't rush her, knowing that healing comes step by step.

One evening, Nyota found a child's drawing in her notebooks: a girl in tears, a tall man standing behind her. She stared at the image for a long time, then burned it in a metal box. Watching the paper burn, she whispered, "You no longer possess me."

At the next session, Mrs. Owens asked her, "Do you want to forgive him?"

Nyota froze. Forgiving sounded like betraying.

"Why would I do that? He destroyed me."

Mrs. Owens slowly nodded.

"Forgiveness doesn't excuse. It liberates. It says, 'I no longer let your poison live in me.'"

Nyota looked down. She remained silent, but that night she wrote in her journal: *"I don't want to forgive him. But maybe I don't want to carry him anymore either."*

Therapy became a rhythm. Some sessions left her trembling, others made her feel light, as if clouds had cleared. Every time, she emerged stronger than before.

A heartbreaking exercise was the "empty chair." Mrs. Owens pointed to the chair facing her.

Melancholy Harmonies

"Imagine your abuser sitting there. Say what you've never been able to say to him."

With her throat tight, Nyota let go. "You stole my childhood. You taught me to hate myself. But you will no longer win."

The words first cracked, then ignited. Tears flowed, but her voice firmed. "You are nothing to me anymore. Nothing."

The silence that followed was heavy but victorious. Mrs. Owens whispered, "That is the voice of your freedom, Nyota."

Melancholy Harmonies

At home, while washing the dishes, Nyota found herself humming. Bibi looked up. "That's the song of healing, my child."

Healing was not linear. Some nights, Nyota woke up sweating, convinced she heard footsteps. Then she would murmur the psalm she had learned: *"Even though I walk through the valley of the shadow of death, I will fear no evil, for you are with me."*

Slowly, panic began to subside. In one of the most difficult sessions, Mrs. Owens asked her to imagine her younger self, the nine-year-old girl, crying alone. "What would you tell her now?"

Nyota closed her eyes. She saw the tears of the young girl, her trembling hands. She murmured, "You are not dirty. You are not worthless. None of this was your fault." Then she added, with surprising strength, "You survived, and it's because of you that I am still here."

When she opened her eyes, Mrs. Owens nodded silently, pride in her expression. "That's how healing begins to take root."

Melancholy Harmonies

Therapy started to spread into the rest of Nyota's life. She began writing in a journal every morning before classes, scribbling thoughts that once poisoned her but now flowed onto paper like venom drained from a wound. Words she had feared to face became ink, and that ink became liberation.

Even Tatu, skeptical about therapy, began to soften. During dinner one evening, he murmured between bites of stew, "I don't know what that counselor tells you, but I see it's working. Your laughter sounds like it did before..." He stopped, clearing his throat, unable to say the word.

"Before all this," Nyota finished for him. There was no bitterness in her voice, only quiet acknowledgment.

Her friends also began to notice her re-emergence — not as the old Nyota, but as a new person, tempered by pain and sharpened by resilience.

Music regained a place in her life. At first, she played the piano cautiously, testing whether melodies still lived within her. But soon, the notes flowed with unexpected force, each chord a declaration: I am alive. I am not broken.

Her therapist encouraged her to share. During a community recital, Nyota performed a piece she had composed — a gentle, enchanting melody building into a triumphant crescendo. The audience rose to applaud, but what mattered most were the tears on her own cheeks as she bowed. They were no longer tears of shame but of liberation.

Later, Mrs. Owens approached her backstage. "You've turned your pain into beauty, Nyota. That's what survivors do."

For the first time, Nyota believed in herself.

Over the weeks and months, Nyota began to see therapy not as a place where wounds were exposed, but as a space where healing unfolded piece by piece. She no longer dreaded entering Mrs. Owens's office. On the contrary, she often arrived with a notebook filled with questions, reflections, or insights.

During a session, she murmured, "I don't want my story to define me anymore."

Mrs. Owens gently tilted her head. "Your story doesn't define you, Nyota. But it can shape you. You are more than what happened to you."

These words engraved themselves into Nyota's heart. They became a sort of mantra she silently repeated whenever shame tried to creep back in.

The chapter of therapy hadn't completely closed, wounds weren't entirely healed, but it had given her the tools to live, to rise, and to dream again. She began to envision a future: one where her voice mattered, where her music could tell stories for those who couldn't speak, where her healing could radiate outward.

On the last page of her journal, she wrote: *"I am not what I was made to be."*

Then she closed the notebook, lifted her chin, and took a step toward tomorrow.

Nyota was among the few children to survive abuse with minimal mental, emotional, and physical damage. She is now an extraordinary adult, a university graduate, and a talented musician.

However, other children in similar situations have been severely affected by trauma that persisted into adulthood. Nyota helps other victims recover from crises and

Melancholy Harmonies

flashbacks. Her resilience and compassion are remarkable, a true source of inspiration for other children.

Parents call on her to console and comfort their children when painful, shameful memories resurface. The children are haunted by flashes and recollections of their past.

Childhood trauma can have lifelong consequences, but Nyota has overcome it with astonishing resilience. It is as if she always knew that the world isn't perfect and never will be, because of human nature. Nyota has committed herself to preventing child sexual abuse and trafficking. Her research has shown her that such abuse jeopardizes children's futures and well-being in adulthood and increases their risk of domestic violence.

Years passed, and Nyota became an impressive young woman, but the echoes of her past remained. It took more than a decade for her to look at herself in the mirror without hearing the taunts of her childhood echoing in her mind. For years, she disguised herself with wigs, fearing that without them, the world would treat her like that girl from school.

But time, in its own way, transformed the pain of rejection into self-esteem. One day, without overthinking, she stood in front of the mirror, removed her wig, and looked at herself. She ran her fingers over her forehead, her cheekbones, the rich tone of her skin. She fixed her gaze on her own eyes, searching for something, and she saw it.

She saw the little girl who fought, the girl who felt invisible despite the spotlight. The girl who once believed she had to hide her true self to be loved. And she saw something else too. She saw a survivor, a fighter, a woman who no longer needed to hide.

That day, she went out without a wig. She left her forehead uncovered. She let the world see her for who she truly was — for the first time in years. And for the first time, she didn't care what others thought of her.

Epilogue

Princess Nyota is only twenty-five years old at the time these lines are written, yet she has lived through more than many could endure in an entire lifetime. Born into war, her earliest memories are marked by the sounds of destruction and the heavy weight of fear pressing down on her small shoulders. She knows what it means to leave home, to be uprooted, and to be cast into a world that does not welcome her with open arms. She knows what it feels like to be unwanted, to be viewed with suspicion, to fight for every ounce of respect.

But she also knows what it means to rise. Life never made her path easy. There were nights when pain wrapped around her like a second skin, whispering that she would never be enough. Days when rejection pierced so deeply she thought the wound would never heal. Moments when the weight of abuse threatened to drown her in darkness so thick she believed she would never see the light again.

And yet, she always found her way back. She never returned as the same girl who had been knocked down. Each time life tried to break her, she rebuilt herself into someone stronger.

She learned to turn pain into something greater, something powerful and undeniable. Music became her first refuge. As a child, when words failed her, she let her fingers dance across the piano keys, allowing melodies to speak the emotions she could not voice.

When she felt invisible, she turned to writing, crafting lyrics that revealed her soul in ways her voice never could. Music did not judge her. It did not reject her. It never asked her to be anything other than who she was.

So she surrendered to it. But music was not her only strength. Her mind refused to be still. Her ambition burned brighter than the doubts that tried to consume her. She became unstoppable—an entrepreneur who built success with the same hands that once wiped away her tears. She refused to let her past define her and refused to allow yesterday's pain to dictate tomorrow's possibilities.

Still, despite all she had accomplished, she knew she was not meant to rise alone. She had seen too many children lost in the same darkness she had once fought to escape. She had read sorrow in their eyes and heard the silent cries of those displaced, rejected, and abused. She knew too well the ache of having no anchor, no clear place to belong. And she knew she could not turn away from them.

"Now," she says, "I use my own story as a weapon against pain. I reach out to you who feel forgotten in this moment. I remind you that survival alone is not enough—you can flourish. You can bloom again. You can dream, soar like the eagle, and prosper. Yes, you can! Let my story be a constant reminder: *You can do all things through Christ who strengthens you.*

"I will be your mentor, your guide, the voice reminding you that your past should no longer be your prison. Step out of it, restored and strengthened. One step at a time. One day at a time. Begin today, and little by little, you will get there. This is a journey you must decide to start right now. Go! Rise! A journey of a thousand miles begins with a single step. Take it."

"If it didn't kill you, then you can kill it," she often declares. "That is what I believe. Pain can either bury you or transform you into something indestructible."

Princess Nyota chose her path. She chose to be more than the sum of her wounds. And now, she is ready to show others how to do the same.

Yet, thousands of miles away in her homeland, Congo, lives are still lost every day in a war that has not yet spoken its final word. On June 27, 2025, the United States brokered a peace agreement between the Democratic Republic of Congo and Rwanda, opening a fragile road toward development in the Great Lakes region of Africa. The very next day, the mayor of Washington, D.C., declared June 30 to be "Congolese-American Day," a call for world powers to build bridges, not walls, between themselves and developing nations.

Nyota will certainly use such moments, during her conferences, to amplify the voices of victims, voices silenced by gunfire, whose cries from rape and abuse still echo beneath the noise of war.

REFERENCES

- Germain-Robin, F., & Namujimbo, D., *La grande manipulation de Paul Kagame*, Arcane, Tarbes, 2023, 375 p.
- Mukwege, D., *La force des femmes*, Gallimard, Paris, 2021, 400 p.
- Onana, C., *Holocauste au Congo. L'Omerta de la communauté internationale*, L'Artilleur, Paris, 2023, 504 p.

ABOUT THE AUTHOR

Jeanine Banza is a born-again Christian, deeply passionate about family issues, especially youth. She is a nurse living in the United States, originally from IRSAC Lwiro in South Kivu, Democratic Republic of Congo. She studied nursing at the Catholic University of Louvain and later pursued public health at the School of Public Health in Brussels, Belgium. A mother of three, Jeanine balances her nursing career with entrepreneurial and philanthropic endeavors alongside her husband.

Made in the USA
Coppell, TX
07 March 2026